The Baker And Malachi

By C.A. Fiebiger

A Novel

Photographs@ MNHS

Printed by Createspace

ISBN-13: 978-1491291078

ISBN-10: 1491291079

Cover art work by Gary Markley

Dedicated to:

The People of my hometown- St. Paul.

Contents

Chapter One- Almost Christmas

"Good night, Ned. Are you ready for Christmas?", sung Olga Sorenson, Sven Tschida's future daughter in law, as he picked up his hat from the tree and put on his coat.

Ignoring her question, he replied softly, "Good night, Olga", and stepped outside. He had not thought about Christmas yet. Ned Oelker, the best baker Sven ever had, walked down the steps and around towards the corner at Maryland in the cold crunchy snow of his 60th winter. He lifted his vest pocket, pulled the chain, flipped open the case, and looked at his well-worn, but trusty watch. It was already half past four. He had to hurry or he wouldn't be home in time to get ready to hear the beginning of the game.

Tschida's Bakery was on Rice Street and the snow was piled up on the sidewalk so far and high, it made it hard for him to move. As always, the wind had pushed it up next to the building as it fell. His limp was more noticeable today and he hobbled as fast as he could as he made his way past the hockey rinks in Sylvan Park. The snow swirled around him, glistening against the sun as it began to sink in the winter sky. "Get out of the way old man," yelled one of the kids as the puck shot past him over the bank of snow the kids used for boards. He did the best he could to move away from them and he just raised his cane in recognition of the Carlson kid who yelled out, "Hi, Mr. Oelker," and waved with it as he left the park.

"I wish I didn't need the cane anymore," Ned muttered to himself. But, he had resigned himself to the fact that he'd need it the rest of his life. He had fallen six years ago during the game at St. Bernard's. It was slippery that night and he had received an emergency call on Father McCarthy's phone from his wife, Suzie, saying she needed help and that she wasn't feeling well at all. He started to leave, but he never made it. He fell so quickly and saw… what was it? He figured it was just a hallucination. Was it- an angel? Naw! It moved so fast, like a blur of radiant blues, reds, and yellows. It must not have been anything like that! Suzie had a heart attack and died while Officer Andy Malone took *him* to the hospital that December night in 1938. Darn leg! And he never had gotten over it, either physically, or emotionally. The whole thing haunted him and Ned visited Suzie at Calvary Cemetery as often as he could, never forgiving himself for his inability to save her.

Ned was a kind, soft-spoken man. He was proud he had voted for Frank Kellogg for senate. He really didn't get involved in much of anything however, and tried to keep to himself, but those that knew him, loved him. His parents had come from Germany in the 1880's and soon after he was born as a US citizen, and he was proud to be so. Ned never had any children. But, his sister Ingrid lived in Minneapolis and she had four girls. She married a Norwegian named Nordstrom. He owned a hardware store and Ollie devoted all his time to his business. Consequently, they never had much time for him. Ned was lucky if he even received a call from her at Christmas. He wondered if that would be the case- this year! Just in case, he had bought the girls each a candy cane. That's all he had thought about Christmas so far this year. He hoped he could deliver!

As Ned turned the corner past the park there was a sudden "boom" and flash of light coming from the railroad yards off Maryland. He jumped in reaction to the noise and his heart did a paddy-pat. Each time something like this happened it took him back to France, the trenches and the war. "Wow", he exclaimed and went on toward his door putting those unpleasant thoughts out of his mind. Not only did Ned struggle with the emotions and pain of the past, because of it all, he struggled with his faith: Faith that God was really there for him; faith that there was room for a man like him in heaven; faith that he was- good enough.

When he got to his door on Rose Street, Max Scheming, the only Jewish neighbor he had, was waiting for him. "Hello Ned, did you bring me the loaf of rye?" Ned didn't reply, but just pulled the loaf, crinkling in its white wax paper bag, out of the long side pocket of his coat and threw it to him.

"What, you are in a hurry?" Max asked. As he did, the screen door slammed and Ned was gone. Now suddenly, being in a foul mood because of his leg, Ned muttered under his breath, "Neighbors." Even though Ned wouldn't admit it, Max was his best friend. They had gotten pretty close over the years. They depended on each other. Both men were widowers. Both men had no children. Both men were angry about the war. Neither of them thought we should be there. Neither of them thought we were helping the Jews. Neither of them did anything about it even though Max had relatives in Europe. It was the one thing that kept Max strong in his Jewish faith. He prayed for the salvation of his people and went to synagogue when he could drum up a ride. There weren't many Jews on this side of town. Nor in St. Paul for that matter! But to his credit, he lived a pious life. The neighbors knew what he was and he them. And they respected each other's beliefs. Ned would do anything for him, but hoped he would come to know Jesus.

Ned took off his hat, threw it toward its' customary hook and missed, put his coat on the chair, and sat down right there by the door so he could take off his boots. He quickly grabbed the newspaper to make sure what time the game was scheduled to start and threw it down into the box where all the other recycled items went. This was Roosevelt's war! Being a pacifist, he hated it and Roosevelt lied. Not only did he have to go without, but now he had to save all this junk, too. He thanked God he worked at the bakery where at least he got some things the rest of the public didn't. But worst of all, half of the teams, (the strong, young guys like he was in 1914) were off fighting somewhere. Baseball, football, hockey, even basketball had felt the demands of this awful mess. Except for the high school teams of course!

Ned was a big fan of the local high school teams. Washington High was close enough it should have been his favorite. But, he had gotten into an argument with the basketball coach, (what's his name?), Schneider, one time when they had played West St. Paul and that ended that. He now rooted for St. Bernard's, even though he wasn't always at mass on Sundays and even though they didn't always have the best of teams. Father McCarthy had said that if Ned came to church as often as he came to the games, he would go to heaven for sure. Ned wasn't so sure.

He turned on the radio to let it warm up and started a pot of coffee. By the time he did that, WCCO was beginning the St. Paul Saints hockey pre-game show. He wasn't hungry, so Ned went to the attic door, flipped the light switch, and slowly went up the stairs. He looked around for the Christmas decorations. Suzie had loved Christmas. There were tons of decorations. But she had one special box of the "good" ones and that's what Ned searched for. He always bought a tree, even if it was on Christmas Eve, the ugliest small one he could get at half price-or less! He was a frugal man. "Man its dusty up here," he said out loud. He found the decorations and one strand of lights. Pushing aside a cobweb, Ned saw the tree topper, an angel made with real feathers Suzie had collected and put together. It was blue, red, and yellow. She called it Malachi. He could never figure that out, but she had told him that Malachi meant, "Messenger". So, he picked it up and placed it atop the box. He carried them down slowly. Trying to navigate stairs with a box in his hands and a cane was somewhat of a problem for him, but he made it without dropping them or toppling down the rickety staircase. When he got downstairs the game was about to start and the coffee was hot. Sitting down, he sipped his coffee and relaxed for the first time since he got home.

Setting Malachi aside, he opened the box and looked at the decorations on top. The balls with painted snow scenes were his favorites and they had come from Germany, passed down from Suzie's mother. Some were 50 years old and some even older. They brought back memories of good Christmases with her; The Christmas she had given him his watch after saving for a year; The Christmas he had worked overtime and bought her the refrigerator so she could get rid of the ice box. And- all the times they had turned on the radio and listened as they decorated the tree. He missed her and in these ornaments he could go back to Christmases with Suzie. He wondered when he would have the time to go get the tree. He'd have to plan that.

The announcer woke him from his daydream. He turned up the radio. He almost never missed a single game on his Philco, scratchy as it was to listen to. But, there was one time he did though. A tube had fried with a resounding sizzle just ten minutes into the last game of the World Series. The Yankees won. So, he had gone to bed early and had said to Max, "The Yankees are going to win 7-6". And indeed, he was right. Max, who came over like most evenings the Yanks were on to listen to the game with him, had just dismissed it. But, Ned knew. He had never been wrong about a sports score- that is.

"It", had begun just after his fall. Officer Malone had said when Ned slipped to the ground, he hit his head on the cornerstone of the church, which coincidently, was laid the same month and year Ned was born, August, 1884. And ever since, at least if the game had started, he always *knew* the outcome of the game he was listening to. He didn't notice it at first. He got kind of tired if the games went to ten o'clock and went to bed. But each time he did he'd say, "I bet Cleveland wins", or the White Sox, or whoever. And he was *always right.* When he had done this a dozen times or so, he began to predict the score, and low and behold the first time-he was right! He was kind of proud of himself. But then he did it again and again, and once more. Suddenly, he was starting to get a little bit afraid, but-why? It didn't hurt anybody. He thought to himself, 'Did I just predict this, or did I *determine* it?' He didn't know. And he sure didn't want to. So he just kept it all to himself and watched, listened, and remembered the vision of the angel. But did that have anything to do with it? Tonight the Saints were behind 3-2 in the third period and he just said, "They haven't got a chance tonight," and went to bed. The next morning there on the front page of the sports section the headline read, "Saints lose again 4-2".

Chapter Two-Nabbed!

Ned went in to work in a chipper mood. He had gotten out of his feeling sorry for himself from the day before. Sometimes when all the events of the past came to him this time of year, he just got a little owly and he had no one to take it out on. When he got there Sven welcomed him.

"Gud morning Ned!"

"Good morning Sven! Is Olga here yet?"

"Oh- ya. She in da front."

Ned walked to the front, cane leading the way with its customary thud, thud, thud.

Olga heard it. "Good morning, Ned," she sang, always in a good mood.

"Olga, I'm sorry I was in such a mood yesterday."

"Oh, don't worry about it."

"Thanks Olga." Ned looked at the bakery cases to see what was in them and went back to help Sven. "Say Sven, are you going to St. Bernard's to watch the match there tonight? "

"Who's bowling?"

"Stahl House and St. Bernard's!"

"Oh ya, I forget! I will be dare for sure, don't ya know!"

When the Stahl House gang came to St. Bernard's to bowl, the competition was fierce. Father McCarthy would even say a prayer at mass the night before just to make doubly sure the team would have the upper hand. Ned would get rather upset every time they'd come, just because of Ben Egger. You see, Ben was a member at St. Bernard's, but he bowled with the Stahl House gang. What a traitor! But most of the guys stayed arms length away from Ben, because back in the thirties he used to box professionally. And he was tough. They knew they would have an easier time if Ben would just come back to their team.

Ben had left in a huff one Sunday after leagues were done, because he caught Tim Wendt cheating on the scores. Ben never spoke to Tim again, even though he usually sat in the next pew up from him at Sunday Mass. And Ned just never let Ben alone about it. He'd tried to speak to him the week before Easter last year, but Minnie, his wife, got in his way and by the time he got close enough Ben was out the door! Minnie was always there for Ben. She was always the peacemaker and Ned respected her for it. And not only that, but next to him, she had the best poppy seed bread on the block. And Ned knew she was right this time and that Ben just needed time to cool off.

Ned went over to the lanes about two-thirty pm just to get a good seat. If he didn't get there early, he'd have to sit in the back. Being only five feet tall, Ned didn't have a chance to see a thing if he didn't. Some of the bowlers were already there talking to their cronies and trying to put aside the butterflies formed in their stomachs. This wasn't just another match. This was *the* match of the year. If St. Bernard's won they'd clinch the title for the first time in a decade. And Ned didn't have a clue. As always, the game had to be ten minutes out in order for Ned to know the outcome. Oh, how he was on the edge of his seat as big John O'Leary the electrician picked up his ball and hurled it down lane six to begin what was to be the beginning of Ned's nightmare!

Ned rarely drank. He knew the effects of alcohol on a man. And St. Bernard's had a no drinking policy. But, there was a liquor store by the barber shop up the street from Tschida's and one of the boys had smuggled in a bottle of whiskey. He offered him a swig. At first Ned declined, not wanting to break the rules and besides, he had to get up early. But he offered him a drink a second time and Ned, looking around to see if anyone of his friends saw him first, took a nip- and another- and another. By the time the two teams had gotten to the last three frames of the match, Ned was feeling no pain. Even his leg felt remarkably well and almost like he didn't even need the cane. But that's what spirits will do to you and Ned was no exception to the rule. Ned suddenly and without hesitation announced to all those nearby, "The Stahl House is going to lose this year. Egger and Kolodziej won't pull it off".

Local thug Evan O'Reilly responded with an, "Oh sure, Ned, and what will you be predicting next year? They're twenty pins down and they don't have a chance!"

"Just you wait and see you ugly Irishman! Why don't you stay on your own side of town?" Ned responded. And rather slowly, he walked out to the coatroom. It was almost ten pm and Ned had to get up early for work at the bakery.

Evan looked after him, blew out a bellowing puff of smoke from his White Owl cigar, and in amazement said to his buddies, "What got into him?" They all smiled and laughed at the sudden outburst from the usually calm and respectable old man. But before Ned had a chance to leave, the match was over, and low and behold the St. Bernard's team was the victor! The roar from the St. Bernard's crowd was deafening. Father McCarthy was jumping up and down yelling all kinds of Irish slang. Evan couldn't believe it! He thought about what Ned had predicted and watched the old man stumble out the door as he left for home.

Evan followed Ned in his car from about a block behind. It was an easy task with the lights on Sylvan Street and. of course. with his limp and cane. As he watched Ned go up the stairs and fumble with his keys, he quickly walked up behind him, and with a cold grasp pushed the door open with a slam. and forced his way into the room with Ned. Startled, Ned said, "Hey what's going on here?"

Evan grabbed Ned's arm and pushed it into an arm lock behind his back and with teeth clenched asked him, "How did you know they would win? I had everything riding on Stahl House. I lost a bundle tonight and I want to know how you knew! Did you have a fix on this?"

Pleading with him Ned responded, "No, no, no fix. I just knew, I just *knew*!"

"C'mon old man tell me or I'll break this arm."

"OK, I'll tell you, but you won't believe me," said Ned.

"Try me," and Evan released the pressure on him.

Ned turned and faced Evan. "Well, it all began when I fell and hit my head and hurt my leg. Ever since, I just *know* who's going to win- no matter what it is."

"You mean you can tell the score of *any* game"?

"Yes, any game as long as it is ten minutes before. Never before that."

"May the saints be praised"! Evan shouted, "I finally found my ticket. C'mon lets be going," he said softer, realizing what he had just done.

Confused, Ned asked, "Now? Where are we going?"

"From now on old man, we are inseparable-best friends". He chuckled and Evan hurriedly led him out the door. Ned saw Max's light on as they got to the sidewalk and he started to yell for help, but it was to no avail as he was pushed into the backseat of Evan's car and the door slammed shut.

Chapter Three- New Space

Sven hung up the phone and looked over at Olga. "He's not dare," he said. "He must be on his vay. I not even see him last night at St. Bernard's."

Ned had not shown up for work and Sven was worried. "This is just not like him," said Olga. "He is never late".

Sven shook his head in agreement and went back to the bread on the table. At six in the morning he was really worried and he called the police. "Ya officer, he never show up", Sven told the cop on the phone. "You check it out? OK, bye," and he hung up. "Vell, I hope he's OK," he said to Olga and leaving Thor the apprentice in the back, the two went to the front of the bakery as the early morning customers were beginning to come in.

But, Ned was not okay. Evan had taken him downtown to the red light district, where pimps and hookers were the norm, and gamblers came to back doors to give their numbers to their bookies on the sly. Even after the cleanup in the late 30's some of the cops still found room to let the mob come over from Chicago. The "Outfit" was big and was going to try to make its mark here, too. But, just a little at a time and they only let one "boss" come over to get started. But no one talked about it, not even the cops because these crooks seemed "legit". Except for Barfuss the Commissioner, who was always on the lookout and still wanted a clean town. He would have none of this!

Ned had not yet woken from the evenings partying and Evan was talking to someone on the phone. "And he knew who was going to win! Yes, I know that's impossible, but that be what he says. I'll be giving him a test today and we'll be seeing how he does. Goodbye," and he slapped the phone down on its receiver. "Get up Ned," he shouted as he walked toward the bedroom. "It's time to be getting up!" and he slapped Ned on the back.

The baker slowly sat up and grabbed his head in his hands. "Ooohhh," he groaned. "What happened last night? And what am I doing here?"

"You be me guest dear friend," said Evan, and he handed him a cup of coffee.

"Your guest?" he quizzed.

"For a long time, this is your room."

"My room? What is this about Evan?"

"Last night you knew the outcome of the match. You told me how you "know" who is going to win and unless you do, you'll never see the streets again."

"But I was drunk! You believed an old, drunken man?"

"I sure did and by gosh I plan on seeing some results!", and Evan shut the door to Ned's new room. A snap on the lock told Ned that Evan was serious and he planned on him staying there.

Bewildered and hung over, Ned shook his head, drank his coffee, and wondered what he was going to do next.

There was a knock at eight am on Max's front door and a resounding "Police", as he undid the latch and the hinges squeaked open.

"Yes, what can I do for you Officer Malone?" Max responded.

"Have you seen, Ned, your neighbor? He never showed up for work this morning and he doesn't answer his door," asked Andy.

"I haven't seen him today, but he gets up early for work and I seldom see him go. But, late last night just after I went to bed, I did hear something unusual. I thought I heard a car door slam and Ned doesn't have a car. He hasn't driven for years. It was too early for him to go to work at that time anyway. Hey, maybe he was getting home from the match at St. Bernard's?! Maybe someone gave him a ride home."

"Maybe so, Max", replied the cop, "but nothing else unusual? See anyone or anything else?"

"Not a thing, Andy. Say, how's the wife?"

"Just fine. Thanks for the information."

And the cop left. As he walked to the gate he noticed a cigar butt in a rut by the street. He bent over and picked it up. He recognized the brand- White Owl.

Officer Andy Malone was the most dedicated cop the department had. He was second-generation Irish. He only had a little Irish flare to his voice. And he lived in a predominantly German-Italian part of town and everyone loved him. He was a "good cop". He moved away from the "bad area" of town when he got the job and was able to afford what God had blessed him with a little farther out. He did his job well and was up for promotion to detective. They even let him have his own desk, which was unheard of while you still had a beat. Some of the guys were jealous, but they all liked Andy and didn't say much. They knew what was coming. He deserved it.

When he got back to the station, Malone reported to Capt. Peterson. Capt. Peterson had been there for as long as anyone could remember; a sole survivor of the shake ups, mostly because he was the only other honest cop! He knew everybody and his brother. "Tell me Captain, is there anyone we know who goes to St. Bernard's that smokes White Owls?"

"No one, but half the Irishmen in the place. Why?"

"When I left Ned Oelker's place today, I found a butt in the gutter. His neighbor said he might have gotten a ride home from someone who was there with him. That's all."

"Any other leads?" inquired the Captain.

"Not much. But I wonder what happened to him. I'd like to go back and take another look."

Approvingly, Capt. Peterson said, "Go ahead. You never know, Andy."

"And I might ask around at St. Bernard's, too." Peterson looked down at his paperwork and nodded his head as Andy went out.

Chapter Four- A New Game

After his cup of coffee, Ned didn't really feel any better. It had been a very long time since he tied one on like this. He could hear a radio on in the other room and except for that, he didn't know if he was alone or not. He didn't like the idea of being in a strange room where he didn't know where he was. He looked to see what time it was, but his watch was gone. He didn't have a window in his room, but he could tell it was beginning to get dark. He finally heard footsteps and a voice he recognized as Evan's came from the other side of the door. "Look at this Ned and write down what you think. I'll be back for it later." He picked up the scrap of paper Evan had slid under the door.

"But I told you I don't, no, I *can't* tell you until ten minutes before the game begins!" he shouted back through the door.

"Give it a whirl and I'll be back in a couple hours with a wee bit of food for you."

"Stupid Irishman!" Ned railed. He crumpled up the scrap of paper and threw it in the corner of the room.

Head in his hands, Ned sat on the edge of the bed until it was so dark he could barely see a crack of light under the door. He got up, followed it to the doorway and felt the wall up to where a switch would be. He pushed the button and on came a single bulb hanging from two wires in the center of the room. In the corner was another door, which he assumed, led to a bathroom. As he needed to relieve himself, he went to explore this new addition to his environs. It had the bare necessities and it would do. On the way back to his bed he saw the scrap of paper he'd thrown in the corner. Ned picked it up again and put it in his pocket. He noticed his leg didn't feel as bad today. And that his cane was gone, too!

Sitting on the bed, Ned figured it had to be about six-thirty by now. He was tired, and tired of this situation. He pulled the scrap of paper from his pants pocket. On it was the names of two teams, the Gophers and the Wolverines. "That's right they play tonight," Ned said to himself. Minnesota had a good basketball team this year. But Wisconsin had been their nemesis for years. Ned heard that the bookies downtown were giving the Wolverines the edge by three points. Ned never bet. He wasn't a gambling man. He'd been tempted since this "gift" came along, but he never went out to act upon it. He just wasn't like that. But Evan sure was, and now he was held prisoner by a greedy opportunist. 'Maybe if I just play along and do this for him this one time he'll let me go home', he thought to himself- typical pacifist thinking. By now the game had almost started for sure and Ned took the pencil from the table and wrote a number by each team name. To his surprise, the Gophers would win, 68-52. He slipped the paper under the door, switched off the light and went to bed. He never did get his meal.

Ned never heard Evan come in that night. He always slept soundly. He woke up the next morning to howling in the next room. Suddenly, the latch on the door was undone and the door flew open. Evan came in and threw the Pioneer Press across to Ned as he lay on the bed. "Look at that! You did it!"

"Did what?" asked Ned as he opened up the early edition.

"You predicted the right score!" And sure enough, there on the sports page cover it was, "Gophers upset Wolverines 68-52".

Ned nodded. "Now can I go?" he asked.

"Are you kidding?" replied the smiling Irishman, "I think your time here has just begun." And turning around he closed the door and snapped the lock shut.

"Hey, I'm hungry," Ned shouted after him.

"Alright! I'll be going to get you something with me winnings," and Evan laughed as he left.

Ned wondered about the bakery and what Sven, Olga, and Thor must be thinking about him. What he didn't know is that not only were they thinking about him, they were doing something as well. Sven had called Officer Malone at the station and spoke with him about Ned's disappearance and what Andy had found. "Vat did you find dare, Andy?" asked Sven.

Andy told him, "not much", but asked Sven if there was anyone else who had heard from Ned.

“Dare is no von else,” answered Sven, “He has no family except his sister and she live in Minneapolis. Day don’t talk much ya know.”

“Is there any way I could get into his apartment?”

“Ja. You could ask his neighbor, Max. Dats his only other friend.” When Sven hung up, he went to his room upstairs to take a break. He had not been sleeping well since Ned disappeared. He got on his knees. A man of deep spiritual conviction, he said a prayer. “Lord, I pray dat no madder where my friend Ned is, you are dare wid him, too. Bring him home to us safe. Amen.” Sven was a second-generation American son of a Swedish mom and a German dad. His father Karl had started the bakery when he was ten. Even so, he had an accent. His mom didn’t want to assimilate into the American way of life. So, she spoke Swedish as much as she could. Karl tried to teach him German, but no matter, because he still had an accent. His dad died in WWI and his mom shortly thereafter, but he had worked every day with them and knew his trade well. Ned was their friend and after the war, Sven gave him a job and taught him everything he knew. Sven was loyal to his friends.

As Officer Malone stepped into the front gate of Max’s yard the dog over the fence barked loudly at him. Andy wondered about that. Where was he the night Ned disappeared? He’d have to find out. Max had heard the dog that night, but never paid much attention because, “He barks all the time, and you just get used to it”.

“Did Ned ever give you a key to his house Max?” asked Andy.

“No, he never did. But he did put one under the mat if he knew he might be gone for awhile. I just use that if he needs me to.”

“I’ll check it out and thanks, Max.” Andy walked over to Ned’s and noticed it had snowed since Ned’s disappearance. The walk had not been shoveled and when he tried to lift the mat by the door it stuck to the ground. He gave it a good kick and when he did the key went flying out from under it and went straight into a bank of snow! “Oh no!” he shouted. By the door was an old, ratty broom and he picked it up to try to find the key. But in the corner of the entry was- Ned's cane! He couldn't believe what he saw. What was that doing there? He might have forgotten it when he went in, but what about when he left? Ned would never leave that behind. It was more than odd. Now he had to find that key and he didn't want to have to go to the judge to get a court order, even if the evidence was starting to pile up. But, what did it prove?

Andy quickly swept toward the spot he last saw the key, but he knew he had to be careful or he'd watch it fly into the snow one more time. He softly swept farther and farther out into the yard and suddenly- there it was! His Irish heritage showed through as he proclaimed, "Praise be!" He picked it up and as he turned the latch on the door the phone began to ring. It had rung about six times when he quietly lifted the receiver off the hook. He listened, "Hello Ned? Are you there?"

"Who's this?" Andy inquired.

"It's Hal. Who's this? That's not you, Ned, is it?"

"Hal who?" Andy asked again.

"Hey, I don't know who this is, but what are you doing answering Ned's phone?"

"Hal, are you Ned's friend? This is Officer Andy Malone and I'm here investigating Ned's disappearance."

"His what?" Hal asked in shock.

"No one's seen him for the last two days, what are you calling about?"

"I'm a buddy of his. We served in WWI together. We don't see each other often, but when I know I'm going to be in town from Illinois, I give him a call. I was just going to set up a time when I could come by."

"Is there anything you could tell me about him that might help?"

"I'm sorry officer, but I don't think I'd be much help. He's kind of quiet you know and he likes sports, but like I said, we haven't talked much lately. Except, you know, I did get a funny letter from him a couple months ago. He wanted to tell me about something that was bothering him. Something about a gift he got. I don't know what he meant."

"Thanks, Hal. Do you have a way for me to contact you if I need to ask you any more questions?"

"You can contact me at the American Red Cross in Minneapolis for the next week. I'm going to see the senior director, Stan Peters, there."

Andy looked around. He didn't see anything unusual except the door to the attic was open and there on the kitchen floor was Ned's watch. The dial was cracked and the time had stopped at 10:10!

Chapter Five- Evil Evan

Evan took the pile of cash from his bookie and smiled as he lit a cigar and said, "I've finally paid you off and I can promise you- I'll never be beholding to you again!"

"Sure Evan, we'll see," said bookie Vic Vitale with a laugh. An old timer straight from Sicily, Vic was the first to wonder how Evan had done what he had done. To pick the winner of the game for Evan was a feat in itself, but to know the exact score was something else. He'd keep an eye on this one.

Vic used the pharmacy as a front, with a store manager and a real pharmacist! The building was in the perfect location by the Hamm's Brewery. When the second shift got off, he could expect the regulars to come in with their "scripts"! The bosses in Chicago made him keep it quiet- real quiet. It was nothing like back in the old days. Now- everything had to be legit. And that was a direct order from the Godfather.

Evan walked out the back door of the pharmacy and went over to Ma Klein's Kitchen. The fiery redhead had bought the old rail car from Mr. Oscar Ferguson when he retired from the railroad and turned it into a diner. She had done a great job on it, with black and white tile floors, stainless steel rails and chairs, and lots of mirrors. The stout Catholic women watched O'Reilly as he made his way to the counter. She never really liked him and always had one eye upon him whenever he came around. "I'll have two corned beef sandwiches to go Claire," Evan announced. That was her name- Claire. Claire Klein. It had a ring to it, but everyone called her Ma, and those that called her Claire, got a raised eyebrow and a sour look. And this time was no exception. She didn't acknowledge him, but gave the order to the cook via her order pad and pencil, which she placed behind her right ear. Evan sat at the counter and took a look around the diner to see who was there. Back in the end booth sat Andy Malone on a coffee break.

When Evan saw him, he turned his back and picked up the paper. Andy was through and made his way to the register to pay. "Thank you Officer Malone," Ma said to Andy as he handed her the ticket and a little extra for a tip.

"You are welcome, Ma," replied Andy. Just at that moment the ash from Evan's cigar fell from the end and landed right on the floor in front of him. Andy looked at Evan with a smile and said, "Smoking White Owl's now Evan, are we?" Evan was startled that Andy knew he was there. But this was no coincidence that Andy Malone was in Evan's favorite restaurant that morning.

"It's been a long time since I've seen you here Officer Malone. What be bringing you to the slums?"

"Just a little official business, Evan. An old gentleman by the name of Ned Oelker has been missing for a couple of days and we are trying to locate him. You wouldn't have happened to have seen anything would you now, Evan?"

Evan's face turned white as a ghost and just then Ma brought his order to the counter. "That will be One-Ten, Evan," said Ma and before he answered Andy, Evan quickly handed her two dollars and headed out the door. "Wait for your change, Evan," yelled Ma, but he was already gone. "I wonder what got into him?" Ma said to Andy.

"Yes, I wonder. Say Ma, what did he order?" asked the cop.

"Two corned beef sandwiches. Why?"

"Two, huh? Oh- just thinking again. Goodbye, Ma."

When Evan got to his place, he quickly closed the door and glanced out the window to see if anyone tailed him before he drew the blinds. He was visibly shaking and it wasn't from the cold. He thought about what had just transpired at Ma's all the way home. And he now had doubts about his plan to keep Ned there any longer. What was that cop up too? Did he really know anything or was he bluffing? Evan could always take his guest back to Detroit with him and visit his uncle until the heat was off. But, he thought, he would just wait and see what happened and do what he needed when the time was right. He didn't want to lose this man, this baker- with a gift. And he wouldn't *kill* the goose that laid these golden eggs either!

Evan opened the door to the Frigidaire and grabbed two Schmidt's. He set one on the table, grabbed one of the sandwiches and opened the latch on Ned's room. "It's about time," Ned said as he grabbed the sandwich and ravenously tore into it while he motioned for Evan to open the beer for him.

"Hey, hey, old man, wait, sit down, while I tell you a little story during lunch." Ned sat in the only chair. "You see, while I be getting your meal, I happen to run into an officer of the law and he says to me he does, "You haven't happened to have seen an old gentleman by the name of Ned have you?" Well, I don't think I be needing that kind of question. So I got out of there real quick. But don't you go getting any kind of ideas that anyone is going to save you, because they're not!" With that Evan got up, picked up Ned's beer bottle, and in anger hit him on the side of the head. "And you had better keep up picking the numbers or I'd be afraid what I be doing to you next time!"

Ned hit the floor coughing on the sandwich and blood oozed from the gash on his temple. Evan kicked him in the side and laughed all the way to the door. He turned around, looked at Ned and left the room. Ned just lay there, dazed, bloody and confused. Finally and mercifully, he passed out. About an hour later Ned began to waken, at least he thought he was waking up because he looked across the floor and saw in the fog of his mind a strange sight. An angel, glowing bright in the corner of the room, began to speak. "Do not be afraid, Ned. I am Malachi, the angel you saw the night of your fall. I am *your* angel, Ned. I will not let Evan harm you anymore. Trust me." Ned fell back into sleep.

Chapter Six- Religious Rivalries

Saturday nights, the bakery hummed with activity as Sven and his apprentice, Thor, prepared all the goods for the Sunday morning rush. There used to be Blue Laws in town, but not anymore. Things change in times of war. So the day off shifted to Monday instead of Sunday. Sven didn't like that too much and neither did the rest of the crew. Not to mention Pastor Wenck at Concordia Lutheran. Pastor liked Sven and he wanted to see him each Sunday. However, the only times he saw him now was on Wednesdays for Lent and Advent, and on Monday night bowling at St. Bernard's. Concordia was scheduled to bowl against St. Francis's there this week and Pastor Wenck was ready. His average was 209 now and he couldn't wait to show those Catholics a thing or two on the lanes!

Pastor called on Sven at the bakery just five minutes before quitting time on Sunday. Sven was putting the few rolls that were left over from the days sales into the case that were to be day-old for tomorrow, when he heard the cow bells ring as Pastor came in the door. "Pastor Wenck, gud afternoon! So nice to see you! Vat would you like?" asked Sven.

"I'd like two of those Danish rolls there Sven. And I'd like to see you in church next week, too!" replied the middle-aged pastor.

"Ja, I know Pastor, but I could only come once in a while even when I had Ned. But now widout him, I don't know vat I vill do!" said Sven as he threw up his hand over his head.

"Oh yes! That's right. I heard that Ned was missing. You still haven't heard anything about him?" asked the clergyman with great concern.

"No, vee haven't. And I am gettin very voried," said Sven as he put the rolls in a white bakery sack and handed them over the counter to the pastor. "Dees are on me, Pastor."

"Oh thank you so much, Sven. But, you didn't have to do that."

"It is my honor and privilege to do so," said the baker as he wiped the top of the counter with a cloth and sent crumbs flying all over the floor.

"Well Sven, if you hear anything, or if there is anything I can do to help, just let me know. I'll see you tomorrow night at the bowling league, won't I Sven?"

Pointing a finger at Carl, Sven said, "You betcha."

Pastor Wenck adjusted his scarf, pulled his hat down farther on his bald head, and went out the door into the cold night air. Sven looked at the pictures on the wall and smiled. Smiling back at him was Ned and his wife Mary. "I hope I don't lose Ned like I lost you Mary." He locked the door, picked up his broom, and shut off the lights.

On the other side of town, Evan came back and found Ned still on the floor. "Get up!" he shouted. Ned didn't move. "Get up!" he yelled one more time and Ned's body began to stir. It was with extreme pain he lifted his head off the floor and turned to see who was yelling at him. He sat up and felt his head. "I be needing you to give me some more numbers, old man. Here are the teams; two NHL games, and for my own personal satisfaction the outcome of the match between the Lutherans and Catholics."

"Give me a minute, please. I don't feel so well."

"You can get better after you do this. Make it snappy," Evan snarled.

"What time is it?" he asked.

"It be almost half-past seven, Ned, and the games start at seven-thirty. Hurry!" said Evan in a more reasonable tone.

"Give me the pencil and I'll write it down," said Ned wearily.

Evan took the scores when he finished and helped him up to his bed. "Lie down and get some rest. I think you'll be happy to know you'll be leaving this dreary place shortly if these numbers work out!" With that he left the room and latched the door.

Ned smiled, pulled over his pillow, and now, finally, he had hope. He'd be going home! Maybe... it *was* the angel? Evan smiled as he walked down the stairs. He had plans for this guy and they weren't in Minnesota.

Vic opened the door a crack to look out and seeing Evan, he let him in. Closing up quickly, he went to his table and continued to listen to a hockey game on the radio. Two of his men entered scores on the boards on the wall while one more manned the phone.

"I want to roll over the rest of this on these," Evan said and he handed him the scores and a sack of cash. "There be three-thousand four- hundred in there. If I win, I'll be on Easy Street!"

"Sure Evan," Vic replied, "I've heard that a million times before". The rest of the men in the room laughed.

"You'll see, and I'll be back to rub your noses in it!" Evan retorted, and he slammed the door as he left. Vic wondered if he would be paying out this time. He hoped he wouldn't have to.

Over at St.B's, Pastor Wenck missed the 9 pin and turned with a wince as he went back to dry his hand on the chalk. It was the 8th frame and they were only 4 pins behind the team from St. Francis's. He picked up his ball, which he called "Grace", and walked up to the line. He took aim and let fly with his second shot. It slowly hooked to the left and "smack", down went the 9. The team went wild and cheered. The crowd wasn't so happy, because it consisted of mostly the people from St. Bernard's and they were Catholics. So, when Lance Malishefski, the plumber, picked up his ball to shoot the ninth frame, they cheered and rooted him on. The Pole had come over to America in 1938 just before things got rough. And he was an excellent bowler with an average of 219. He was at 245 and he was on a roll, so to speak. Lance was a lefty, and as he approached his turn, he made the sign of the cross with his right hand and held his ball with his left. His big strong hands almost covered his ball as he took aim. His smooth release was a joy to watch and the ball glided down the lane toward its mark. The sound of a strike is easy to recognize and as he turned to go to his seat he knew he was successful. The St. Bernard's crowd went wild and the noise was deafening. He bowed and with a menacing smile aimed at his opponents, he sat down.

It was Sven's turn next. As he picked up his ball, he noticed Evan had come in. He sat at the snack bar with his friends and a stranger Sven had never seen before. Sven also noticed Officer Andy Malone in the crowd as well. He was glad to see him. Father McCarthy insisted, unofficially of course, that an officer of the law be there when they had these rivalries. One would never know when something "fishy" might occur and the priest would not tolerate it. And besides, Andy wanted to ask some questions.

Sven was in his 10th frame and he was nervous. His score was 235 now and he wanted to do his best and try to strike out the frame. He prayed a short prayer in Swedish and went forward. While he did, Andy Malone was checking out the crowd, but mostly the group at the snack bar. Evan still had not noticed him and Malone was glad of that. So, he kept out of his sight and moved back into the horde.

Sven released what he thought was going to be a strike, but just at the last moment it turned into the king pin and left the 7 & 8. He was disappointed and hung his head as he went back to retrieve his ball. Pastor Wenck called over to him, "Don't worry Sven. Just pick up the spare and we'll be OK. Do your best."

"OK, Pastor," he said and picked the swirling ball up out of the return. "Von more time," Sven said under his breath and he positioned himself for his second shot. He looked intently at the remaining pins, stepped up to his "spot" and stopped. The crowd went silent. Evan whispered to the stranger, "I'll bet you a fin he misses!"

"You're on!" he replied.

Sven took three steps, swung the ball down to release it and as he watched it roll down the alley you could have heard a pin drop! And did they ever! Crash went the two pins for a perfect spare. The crowd roared! "Damn!" exclaimed Evan as he handed the man the fiver. After his last ball the game was tied and it was all up to the last two bowlers, Lance and the Pastor.

Lance was first. With little hesitation and perfect execution he produced two strikes. The third ball didn't have spin however, and he ended with an eight for a total of 283! What a game!

Pastor Wenck was under the gun. Figuratively- that is. He didn't play around and did things matter of factly. His first ball started to stall, but picked up the grove and ended up a strike. He was nervous and delayed for a bit of time before his next ball. He wiped his hands on the chalk cone and dried them on his towel. Sensing this, one of the Catholics in the crowd yelled out, "Stop stalling Pastor. No amount of praying will do it for you this time!" The crowd roared!

"Don't listen to him," Andy Sandvig said, "let's pray!"

Calling them together the four men listened as Wenck said, "Lord only you know the outcome of this game, but if it be your will, we pray that you may be glorified by our witness to you by our victory." Little did Pastor Wenck know that at least two others besides God knew who would win.

Evan watched all these events from the bar, rose slowly from his stool, and said goodbye to his friend. He waited until everyone else was watching intently on the action and quietly slipped out the back door. He didn't want to be there to react when Pastor Wenck threw his last ball because, unbeknownst to them, *he* knew the outcome. He also didn't want them to know that he had bet it all- *against the Catholics!* He couldn't bring himself to bet for the Lutherans, so he did it that way instead. He walked out the door, putting on his gloves as he headed toward the back door of Vic's place. The wind blew and the snow was coming down in buckets. He pushed his hat down to the tops of his ears to block the weather out. In doing so, he didn't notice Officer Malone come out the door a hundred yards behind.

G-2300

Chapter Seven- Big Deal!

Before Evan could reach the back door to Vic's, the phone had already rung to tell the Italian the results of the match. Vic knew what this meant. He'd have to tell the big boss and the boss didn't like this kind of news. He didn't have that much money on hand to pay Evan. Evan had won the two NHL bets and now he had won the bowling bet as well. The grand total came to 65 big ones. Enough to retire! What concerned him the most was the attention this brought to him and his operation there. The boss would be coming over to pay a "friendly" visit on him. Vic didn't like that and that made him just a little bit upset with Evan, to say the least. So when Evan knocked on the door, Vic had two of his men meet him there.

Evan hit the floor as soon as the burly men grabbed him by his arms and threw him across the room. "You big palookas," screamed Evan as he pulled himself up and felt his ear to see if he was bleeding, "What did you go and do that for?"

Vic was right there to help him off the floor, gun in hand. "Who did you pay off to fix the match at St. Bernard's?"

"No one, by me poor mother's grave, I swear no one!" he said pleadingly.

Vic could see the panic in Evan's eyes and he knew he was telling the truth. "Then how did you know?" The Irishman sat down hard in a chair and told him the whole story. The three men standing menacingly over him didn't really believe him this time. It was too good to be true. But before they had a chance to say anything else another knock came at the door.

Vic opened it a crack and took a look out. Before he had a chance to say hello the man on the other side slung it open. It was the big, bosses man, Tony Benito. He was huge. Standing six-four, he tipped the scales at 325. He had boxed pro for 10 years before becoming the bosses' bodyguard. He had to quit because he got too big! He took a look around the room and when he was satisfied things were OK, he motioned outside. In walked two more goons and behind him the boss. "Hello Vic," said the boss.

"Hello, Mr. Howard, glad to see you in town again", replied Vic.

Across the alley, Andy Malone was looking down from the balcony on the neighbors' building. He had seen the bosses' car drive up with Illinois plates. The wind was blowing so hard that the billowing snow made it impossible to make anything out. Besides, he didn't have much cover and now he was covered with snow. He saw the four men go in and the door go closed, and he determined it might be a long wait.

"So this is the man you said was picking the numbers, eh?" Mr. Howard walked over to Evan and stuck out his hand. "Pleased to meet you Evan," said the boss as he took his hand and shook it heartily.

"And who may I have the pleasure to be introducing myself to?" asked Evan.

"Let's just say I'm Vic's business associate, my friend," replied Mr. Howard. "Vic, have you paid Evan his winnings?" he asked.

"Not yet. You know I don't have that kind of money here!" replied Vic.

"Yes. That's right. Tony, bring in my briefcase and we'll pay Evan here. No. Wait. Let's go out to my car and we'll take care of business as we drive Evan home in this storm. How would that be Evan?" asked Mr. Howard.

Smiling, Evan said, "That would be just fine, Mr. Howard. Just fine!"

"Make sure you tell the boss the story you just told me," interjected Vic furiously.

"I'm sure he will, Vic. Won't you Evan?"

"Oh, yes sir. I certainly will," replied Evan strolling out the door glad to be away from Vic.

Over at Evan's, Ned woke up about eleven and listened. He heard nothing. Evan must still be out. He wondered how long *he* had been out. The room was dark now, so he made his way over to the switch and turned on the light. He could see all the blood he had lost there on the floor. Now he knew why he felt so weak. Ned went into the bathroom and after relieving himself, washed up. He felt a little better after this and the sleep he had. But he noticed the growl in his stomach and the hunger he still had. In the three days he had been there, he had not had a lot of food. 'That no good Evan,' he thought, 'I sure wish he'd bring me something to eat.'

Ned was weary. Unsure of his predicament, his only ray of hope was what Evan had said when he left. Otherwise, how long would he keep him there? Would he be there indefinitely? Would he keep him locked up, just using him in order to become rich? Ned didn't know. He wished he didn't know as much as he did! He said a prayer. He wondered about the angel or if it was another hallucination. And if it wasn't, if what he said was true, and what did he say his name was? Malachi? Suzie's, Malachi? He wasn't a tree top angel, that's for sure!

When five men came out of the pharmacy and got in the Cadillac from Illinois, Officer Malone knew he'd have to do something. If they drove away, he'd lose the trail and that would be that. He quickly grabbed the phone on the wall and called headquarters. "This is Andy Malone. I'm on the case and I need a black and white at 224 Payne right away. Is there anyone close to me?"

The Sergeant on duty said to him, "I don't know Andy, but we'll get one over there as soon as we can. Are you alright?"

"Ya, Sarge, I guess that will have to do," and he hung up the phone. Fortunately for Andy, Evan, Mr. Howard, and the two goons sat there in the car at the back of Vic's place for a few minutes talking about things.

Mr. Howard pulled out his briefcase and opened the latches, which snapped open resoundingly. He swung it around and showed Evan its contents. Evans eyes got wide and he smiled from ear to ear. "Its' all yours Evan," said the big boss.

Evan reached out with his gloved hand showing two fingers tips poking through the fabric. "But that be more than what Vic be owing me, Mr. Howard, sir."

"I know Evan," replied Boss Howard, "but, let's talk about *how you were able to pick these numbers Evan."*

"Ah- yes," replied Evan, "that's what I be telling Vic when you came in tonight." Evan related the entire story to Boss Howard and how he had kidnapped the old man. Mr. Howard sat there taking it all in. Evan said, "He calls it his "gift", but I think it be a curse."

Now, Boss Howard's eyes grew very wide. "Tony, ordered the boss, lets drive around a bit so Evan and I can talk some more."

"Right Boss," replied the thug and the car moved slowly forward, tires spinning in the slick, new snow.

Chapter Eight- He Takes it on the Lam

The black and white pulled up to the front of the building just as the bosses' car drove out of sight in the alley. "Thank goodness," said Andy out loud. He ran down the two flights of stairs in leaps and bounds and out the door to car number twelve. He threw the door open and saw Matt Killian. "Hi, Andy. Where to?"

"There's a Caddie going out the alley on Minnehaha. Follow it!" Andy commanded.

"Yes sir!" he replied and the squad car shot off like a sled in the snow. When they got down to the corner they turned right on Edgerton. Lights flickered about two blocks away in the hard falling snow. The thug wasn't driving fast in the snow and it was easy for Matt to keep up with him. Matt had been the best driver at the speedway before his crash in 1939. If it weren't for the bum leg from the incident, he'd have gone off to war with the rest of his friends. Now, he drove as often as he could with the men on the force. Most of the men on the force were like Andy, just old enough, disabled enough, or 4-F enough to not have gone, too. But Matt was in good shape otherwise, and he'd keep up with the best of the crooks! They followed them for close to 5 minutes when, finally, they pulled up to a two-story house down by the flour mill off Albemarle.

Evan got out first and lit up a White Owl, followed by Mr. Howard. "Then we have a deal, Evan?" asked Boss Howard.

"We have a deal, Mr. Howard, sir," replied Evan. Evan handed him the keys to his house, took the briefcase, turned and walked away. Over his shoulder he called, "Oh, Mr. Howard, he may be a bit hungry."

Getting back in the car, and shivering hard enough to knock the snow off his shoulders, Boss Howard said, "Tony, go in and find out what he wants and we'll go get him something to eat."

The bodyguard got out of the car, but caught something out of the corner of his eye. There in the distance, he saw a light reflect off the side of a car down the street. He took a closer look and saw-a cop! He quickly jumped back in the car. "I saw a cop boss!"

"Well don't draw attention to anything. Just pull out and drive away," said Boss Howard.

Andy didn't see Evan walk down the street the other direction because of the blowing snow. In fact, he couldn't see much of anything. He could barely tell there was even a car parked there. "We have to get closer Matt! I can't see anything."

"There they go, Andy," replied the kid.

"Follow them slowly, but don't let them know we are here," and the car crept down the dark Minnesota street.

Evan stopped at the Tin Cups to use the pay phone. He was frozen from the long walk. He ordered a hot Irish coffee. Then he called a cab. "I'll be needing a cab at the corner of Rice and Maryland to take me to the airport," he said. Then he dialed Olga.

She had an apartment by Oakland cemetery. She answered the hallway phone on the first ring like she had been expecting a call. "Where have you been?" she asked in an irritated tone.

"I've made the deal of a lifetime, me dear, and you be welcome to come along," he said bragging.

"Deal, what deal?" she snipped.

"I've sold the old man to Boss Howard and you'll never believe what I be getting for him! *A quarter million*."

"You've *sold* him? How can you *sell* that precious old man?" she scolded.

He hesitated for a second, not expecting her reaction. "Well you don't be needing to speak to me like that, mind you, and I can be surely going alone," he came back.

"Where are you?" she asked.

"I'm going to the airport and if you be willing to come along, we'll be on Easy Street for the rest of our lives. All you be needing to do is be there in an hour." With that, he hung up the phone. No goodbyes. The decision was up to her.

Ned heard the front door open slowly and close with a quiet snap. At first he thought Evan had come home and had brought him some food. But when he didn't hear anything, he wondered what or who it was. "Is that you, Evan?" cried out the prisoner. No response. "Who's out there?" shouted the old man. No response again. After about five minutes of silence he thought maybe he'd just heard a noise and in the back of his mind began to dismiss the whole thing. Then, the latch was opened, and the door swung open ever so slowly. In the doorway stood a small figure and Ned couldn't see who it was because of the dim light and the long coat, gloves, and hat. "Who's there?" inquired Ned. The question went unanswered. Slowly the figure walked toward the table. Ned started to move that direction and the figured stopped. Ned moved back to where he was and the figure began to make its way toward the table again. When it got there it pulled out a bag. Ned smelled food. The bag was deposited on the table. Just as slowly as it had made its way over to the table it made its way back to the door. It closed it, locked the latch and walked away. Ned heard nothing more. He didn't care. He just wanted to eat. He ate the cold cheeseburger in about a minute or less. But it helped. He lay down on the bed and wondered who this mysterious person was. He knew it wasn't the angel. He lay down. Soon, he was fast asleep.

Going down Wabasha, Matt knew the car was not going as slowly as it was the first time he followed it. In fact, he was having a heck of a time keeping up with it.

"Andy, I can drive with the best of them, but this guy can really drive in the snow!" remarked the surprised cop.

"It looks like it. But you had better keep up. He's almost over to the bridge to Wisconsin!" Andy knew that if they made the bridge it was all over. He couldn't even follow them once they got across. They had to try to stop them!

"Pull up and I'll try to get a shot at their tires," said Andy to Matt. Matt put the pedal to the floor and the car's tires spun in desperation. The cars zipped up and down the slick streets as fast as the drivers could manage. But alas, it was no use. The big Caddie just roared up the hill to the bridge and before you know it was safely on the other side in the Badger state. “Damn,” said the cop as they turned around and headed to the Station House.

Chapter Nine- Hal picks up his merchandise

Olga came in the door of the bakery and hung up her coat. "Ver have you been? Olaf has been looking for you," said Sven, "Ve need to start the dough!"

"Oh, I had to finish something before I came," she replied and she took the dough and began her work. Little did Sven know what she needed to finish! Olga and Evan had been more than friends- even in high school. When Olga saw him again at the bakery after he came back from Detroit, her heart had melted. But how could she tell Olaf how she felt? The wedding would most certainly be off and her job would be finished. So, she had decided to hide her affair with Evan and give in to romance. She had now found out the hard way of course. Evan was gone with the money and she was now taking care of an old man he held prisoner! How did she get herself into this? And what was Boss Howard going to do with him? She felt sorry for Ned and had brought him some food. She'd check on him later in the morning, too. Maybe, she could find a way to get Ned free.

Boss Howard spent the night in a cozy cottage on the river in Hudson. The snow draped the roof and drifts were piled up on the North side where the wind blew it up toward the windows. Once in a while the wind would catch a loose shutter and it would flop and make the window rattle. But that never bothered Hal Howard, because he had always liked it there. The waters of the St. Croix seemed to sooth the savage beast within, even when it was winter and the ice cracked and groaned. Hal looked out in a moon lit night to see the river, steam rising as the temperature dropped and he watched chunks of ice float by and congeal in masses like marshmallows in hot cocoa. He called out to Tony, "Hey Tony! Make me some hot chocolate so I can sleep."

"OK, Boss," came Tony's reply.

The hot drink did the trick. When Hal woke, however, he was agitated that he was unable to have picked up Ned and his "gift". 'Some gift', he thought to himself. Hal had paid dearly for it and now he wanted to see its full potential. The first few trial runs seemed to indicate his old friend was 100% on the money every time. So before his two goons were finished with breakfast, he told Tony to warm up the Caddie. "We're going to pick up our "Gift" now boys." And they all had a good laugh about it!

Ned woke to the sound of the furnace clanking in the basement. He thought he felt a little cold. The temperature must have dropped considerably last night, he thought. Or the furnace went out! "Evan!" he shouted several times. But, Evan wasn't there. Nor was the figure he had seen last night. Nothing- just the thumping of the furnace and silence. He went to the bathroom and turned on the hot tap in the tub. Out came hot steaming water that instantly filled the room with billows of hot air. He drew himself a tub of water and got in and soaked for a while. At least one room in the house was warm! He finally took a bar of soap and washed, which felt kind of good he thought, considering he had not bathed in about a week and his wound was still a little caked and raw. But without a razor, he had a scruffy start of a beard, which he considered a terrible addition to his persona. He dried off quickly and put on the same old clothes he had arrived there in the few days before. When he finished, he heard the front door open again. This time he knew it wasn't Evan and it was more than one person.

Ned quietly walked over to the door of his room and listened. Two, no, three sets of footsteps were coming towards his room. The latch was undone and Ned retreated from his position to the other side of his bed not knowing what to expect or who would be there when the door finally came open. Frankly, he was scared and his legs shook. Tony opened the door, but let Boss Howard go in first. "Ned?" Even though it was daylight, the windowless room was still dark, especially after coming in from the sunlight. Hal had to let his eyes adjust. Ned thought he recognized the voice. "Ned is that you?" Hal asked again.

"Hal? Is that you, Hal? Hal! Thank God it's you Hal!" shouted Ned as he maneuvered to the other side of the bed and vigorously started shaking his buddy's hands. "How did you find me?" he asked, "And how did you know?"

"Ned, calm down. Things are fine. Come with me and I'll tell you all about it." Trusting his old buddy, Ned picked up his hat and coat, hobbled down to the Cadillac and got in.

Olga had gone straight to Evans' house as soon as she got off work. She was carrying a loaf of hot bread in a bag under her arm. It caused a bulge under her long winter coat. When she got to the corner of the block, she saw Ned going down to the car at the curb. She also saw the men escorting him there and she didn't like the looks of them. By the time she started walking towards the house they were driving straight towards her! She didn't want them to see her, so she turned and went through a gate and hustled up to the front door of another house, just so she could have her back to them and as soon as they passed by, she quickly turned to see if she could make out anything in the car. She saw Ned in the back seat smiling and talking to a man she had never seen before. Why was he not trying to escape? Why was he being so nice? In his circumstances, you'd think he'd be trying to run away, for crying out loud! It was all perplexing to Olga. She shrugged, turned, and headed home.

Officer Malone stood next to Capt. Peterson's desk and asked him, "Captain, would you allow me to act on a hunch?"

"What's this all about Andy?" he replied.

"Oh, let's just say I know love when I see it and I'd like to follow up on it."

"All right, but don't you dare get me or this department into any trouble or I'll claim you acted on your own!" Peterson snarled.

"Oh, don't worry. Have I ever let you down before?" came back Andy.

"No, not yet, and don't let there be a first time!" yelled the Captain, for Andy was already headed out the glass door of Peterson's office.

Chapter Ten- The "Real" Hal

Ned got out of the car with the hoods and was escorted up to the door of a posh downtown apartment in St. Paul. He'd never seen anything quite like this before and in fact, didn't know a place like this even existed in the capital city. When he got to the penthouse, the elevator door opened up to the nicest digs he had ever been in. Hal took his arm, led him towards the den and took his coat and hat. He handed them to Tony and said, "Come in here. I'd like to show you something." They went down the hall and into a room that looked like a bedroom, but was so wide and open, so lavish, that he really didn't think it could be so. When they went in and closed the door, Tony and the two hoods turned and blocked the entrance on the outside. Ned noticed this, but in turning to look at the magnificent view from the balcony- dismissed it. "Welcome to my home. Welcome to *your* new home, Ned," said Hal, matter-of-factually.

"My- *home*?" Ned didn't think he had heard Hal right.

"Yes, Ned, your home." Ned began to feel a little uncomfortable. "I've seen how you live in that place all alone, working that miserable bakers job, and I thought you might like to come to work for me. Of course this is just one of the perks you'd have and you'd have everything else included as well. Meals, women, you name it," said Boss Hal.

Ned was taken aback. He asked, "And what could I possibly do for you that I could earn all this?"

"Oh there would be a salary included as well, say, fifty-thousand to start, but that's negotiable, of course."

Ned's jaw dropped to the floor. Fifty-thousand dollars! He, no, *no one* makes that much money. Ned asked again, "But what would I be *doing*?"

"Oh, you would just be using the "gift", that's all," said Hal, "and getting lots of sleep!"

Ned began to panic. So that was it! The gift! Ned began to back towards the door. Hal quickly said, "Ned, please, don't make me call Tony. Sit down and let's talk about it. This could be the opportunity of a lifetime- for all of us. Please, let's talk," he reasoned with him.

Ned just stood there frozen. He didn't want to go through what he had just experienced with that Irishman Evan. How could his old buddy do *that* to him? Certainly, *Hal* would let him go. He didn't want to be held prisoner no matter how much he liked sports and he didn't like them that much! He thought quickly and not knowing if he'd go for it, he thought he'd give it a try, "OK Hal, let's talk about it. I don't know if I could work for you indefinitely, but we certainly could give it a trial run."

"Sure Ned. Let's give it a try and see how it goes. I'll set it up and have some of your stuff brought over."

"Thanks Hal," he replied, being convinced the boss had gone for his plan.

But Hal had something else in mind and when he left the room he turned to Tony and said, "Send one of these guys over to his house to get some of his stuff and tell them to be careful. You never know, the cops might have the place covered. And don't you let Ned out of your sight."

Meanwhile, Andy Malone went over to see Max again. This time he wanted to ask for permission to use his upstairs loft for a stakeout. But, Max was hesitant. "What if they come after me?" Max asked excitedly.

"They won't," said Andy, "and if they did, they'd have to come through me to get to you."

"Well, OK Andy, but you'd better be right!"

"If it all goes the way I think it will, I'll be in and out of here so fast *you* won't even know I was here, much less them!"

"Let me get my menorah from the attic," said Max, "I want to set up for Hanukkah before you are up there."

Andy made his way to the second floor window. It was now eleven am. Andy pulled out a pair of binoculars he bought at the Army surplus and placed them on a table. The room upstairs was a typical farmhouse style attic addition. Max needed the extra money during the war and had the room there, but had never used it. One of the girls working at the munitions plant by Phalen Lake had rented it for almost two years. Now that her man had come back injured, they had a bought a new place. Andy moved the dresser over closer to the window to provide an extra screen so he wouldn't be seen. He pushed the frilly shades shut and opened the edges just enough to see out towards Ned's front door which was almost even with the window at Max's.

The Caddie pulled up down the street next to the hockey rink at Sylvan. Tony said to the two goons, "One of you go around back and see if there's anything and the other check with these punks to see if they've seen any cops." Tony just sat in the nice warm car until they made their ways back to report to him.

"I didn't see nuttin, Tony," said the first, and when the other came back he said the same, "These kids ain't seen a ting."

"I'll drive the car into the alley and you two bring out his stuff," ordered the Italian.

"It might take a while and what'll we bring?" asked the bright one.

"I don't care. Just get something. But get his razor and cane for sure, so's the boss don't think you're stupid." And off drove Tony toward the alley.

Chapter Eleven- Hal meets his match

As Olga came in her front door, she heard the landlords' apartment door open. "Hello, Olga," said Mr. Harrigan.

"Hello, Mr. Harrigan, how have you been?"

"Just fine, say, I haven't seen much of you lately. Been out with Olaf again?"

"Oh ja. We have been out by da lake at Como." Mr. Harrigan looked a little puzzled at that answer and she noticed his reaction. It was a bit cold for that. So she quickly said, "We were looking for a nice place to have da wedding in the spring."

"Oh yes, I see, well, see you later!" And off he went out the door.

'Stupid answer,' she thought. Olga was glad to be back at home. She never had brought Evan there. How would she explain that? They had always gone to Wisconsin if they had a free night and if they snuck an afternoon in, they went to Evan's. She sunk into a chair, tossed her head back, and closed her eyes. What in the world had she gotten herself into? She imagined him sitting in a bar in his native Ireland. He always told her about the Crown Bar there in Belfast. That bum! Suddenly it hit her. He might have left a clue as to where he went at his place! So she sprung up out of the chair and flew towards the door. As she put her coat and scarf back on, and turned the knob so the door opened, there blocking her way was Olaf- with a smile on his face!

When the crooks went in they saw all of Ned's decorations in the living room on the floor. "Looks like Ned won't be having Christmas at home this year," said one of them and he shoved the box out of his way. They laughed. But they didn't waste much time. They got the stuff Tony told them to and moved quickly toward the door.

Andy Malone watched them the whole time they were there. He wondered what in the heck they were doing. First they brought out a suitcase, a pillow, and then—a cane. Ned! They had Ned! He picked up the phone and called headquarters. "Andy

Malone here. I need backup on my stakeout! The crooks are about to leave in a Cadillac. Hurry!" Quickly, and with no hesitation, he checked his revolver. He flipped it open and checked to see if it was fully loaded. He never had to use it before, but he figured there would always be a first time. He flew out the back door of Max's place and down the front of the house to Ned's. Drawing his gun, he listened to see if they were still inside- nothing. He heard the back screen door squeak and knew he was too late. Before he had the chance to get back there, he heard the Caddie slowly drive down the alley. The boys from the precinct better hurry or these jokers would get away and they would never find Ned! Andy sat on the stairs and shook his head. By the time his backup got there, they were long, long, gone.

Over at Olga's, Olaf came in the door and hugged Olga, spinning her around off her feet. "Olga, where have you been? I've been trying to see you since the match at St. Bernard's last night! I've got something to show you!" He whipped out an envelope and poured the contents on her living room coffee table. Out flew a stack of money!

In surprise, eyes as wide as silver dollars, Olga asked him, "Olaf where did you get this?"

"Do you remember da Irishman Evan? I think you used to know him from da school?"

Olga was taken aback by the question. Answering slowly she said, "Ya, I think so."

"Vell, last night after I get off of work at the brewery, I make a bet wit him! And look at vat I von! But I didn't tink it would be dis much. Dare is almost tree towsand dollars here!"

That Irishman! Maybe- he wasn't as bad as she thought. Still, she wondered where he had gone- for sure!

When Tony drove up to the apartment building, he noticed another bigger Caddie in the spot where he usually parked. This one had New York plates on it and two of the ugliest goons he had ever seen attended to it. He knew they were Italians for sure! He pulled up to the next parking place and let out the others. As they got their guests belongings out, the guys from back East gave them the eye. Tony unexpectedly caught a glimpse of the wrist of one of the men as he took a drag from his cigarette. The sign! On each of the wrists of members of the mob back in Sicily they were tattooed with the sign; A small octopus facing towards the palm of each member. A Paisano! He turned and faced him and revealed his tattoo! With big smiles and slaps on the back, they gave each other a hug and began a conversation in Italian.

Upstairs, Boss Howard was having his own conversation. "What do you mean you're taking him?" shouted Hal angrily.

"Yes, Mr. Howard, those are my orders," said the neatly dressed young man. "The Godfather requested that you share your new found, "gift", do you call it?"

"He's requested this, did he? This is my property and my friend, and I don't care what he has "requested", and you can tell him so. Now take your fancy New York friends and get out of here."

"He ain't gonna like this," whispered the young man's bodyguard to him as they hurried out of the room.

"I know, but let's get outta here for now." They made their way out the front lobby just as Tony and the boys went through the revolving door. Tony noticed they weren't too happy and wondered what had transpired in the bosses' apartment.

Ned had heard the whole thing in his room. He had only been held like this for a few days and they were fighting over him already! He had to get out of here! If he could only run! Ha! But, how was he going to get away? Hal didn't trust him that was for sure, and besides, he had those guards there! He'd have to come up with a plan.

It was dinner time when they brought him some of his things. And he was hungry again. It seemed like he had not had regular meals these past few days. And he was right. The last time he had anything was the burger the night before. "Say Tony. Could I get something to eat? I haven't had anything since last night."

Surprised, Tony said, "Sure Ned, we can't let our newest roommate go hungry can we?" Tony went out to the kitchen and called the Italian place out in Little Canada. It was a little out of the way, but he liked their food best and the owners were part of the "family". In Italian, Tony told them to get an order of the usual ready to go. Hanging up, he turned to Ned and said, "You'll like this Ned. It's the best around." Ned wanted to eat, but he still wanted to get out of there more.

The food *was* the best Italian Ned had ever eaten. The antipasto was great. The veal was great. The pasta was superb. Still, it really didn't make *Hal* feel better. Boss Howard was fumed. "That no good, second rate mobster had better not fool with me!" shouted Hal at his men. They didn't say a word, but instead concentrated on their meal. "We won't give him the chance! I think we should take a little vacation. Don't you boys? It's a little cold here anyhow."

"Where will we go, Boss?"

"I think we'll go South for the winter," and he laughed as he ate the last of his spaghetti.

Tony raised his glass of wine and toasted, "Salue" and they all smiled. Ned didn't like what he heard and he didn't think he liked the man Hal had become.

Chapter Twelve- Malone hot on the trail

The phone rang at Andy Malone's desk and he put down his pen and answered, "Malone".

"I have some information you might like to hear Officer Malone."

"With whom may I say I have the privilege of speaking?" asked Andy.

"You'll find out soon enough. Just meet me at the Tin Cups at seven-thirty. I'll be wearing a maroon Gophers sweater." The man hung up.

"I wonder what this is all about?" Andy said to himself.

Not to be one to let a lead or some stool pigeon drop through the cracks, Andy made his way to the Tin Cups in the snow. Flakes as big as Zeros fell all around him! It never seemed to stop this time of year!

Andy arrived a little early. He went in quietly and sat in the back so he could see the bar if someone came in and sat down. Seeing as he was off duty and in his civvies, he ordered a Hamm's and said "hi" to the waitress named Alice. She had been there a long time. She also knew everyone and everything going on around the area. She brought his beer and Andy thanked her with a tip. Alice said, "Thanks, Andy" and started to leave.

But, Andy quickly said to her softly, "Say Alice, do you know anything about Evan O'Reilly and where he's off to?"

Alice took a look over her shoulder and whispered, "I haven't seen him in lately, but the scuttlebutt is he went back to Belfast. I've only seen his friend Lonnie in here lately. He's here almost every Thursday when the Fly Tiers meet. In fact, that's him coming in." Andy looked toward the door as Lonnie took off his coat revealing a maroon Gophers sweater. Alice left and Andy waited for Lonnie to come over to his table. He bought a draft and made his way to the back of the bar.

Lonnie looked around, and seeing there were few patrons there, sat down and introduced himself. Andy recognized him as the man that sat with Evan the night of the match over at St. Bernard's. "So," said Andy, "what's this all about?"

Lonnie hesitated a moment and said, "Well, I don't want to be ratting out a good friend of mine, but he's safe now. What he did to the old man is just not right and he needs help."

"Do you mean Ned Oelker?" asked Andy.

"Yes. He sold him to a gambling boss and left the country."

"*Sold him? What do you mean?*" Andy didn't believe his ears.

"That's right. He kidnapped him and sold him to a boss from Illinois for a quarter million, and he's got him downtown in one of those fancy penthouse apartments."

"Why would anyone want to buy an old man like that? What does he have that anyone would want?" asked Andy.

"I couldn't believe what he told me on the phone the first day he had him," said Lonnie. "It seems he can predict sports scores. *Any sports score, as long as it is a game.* Evan made thousands in just a day with him. So he sold him to the guy. It was just another business deal for him." Andy sat there dumbfounded. He didn't know what to ask next, but his time ran out.

Lonnie saw someone and got up and turned his back to the bar. "I gotta go. That'll be twenty bucks." Andy just shoved the bill across to him and Lonnie left.

The pieces were starting to come together now; The Caddie from Illinois; Evan's motives. Andy knew of just two or three apartment buildings downtown that were upscale enough to have penthouses. It wouldn't take long to tract these guys down and free Ned. That is, if they were still there. Some pieces still didn't fit though. What about the girl? One day last August he had seen her with Evan out behind the bakery. It wasn't anything at the time, even a kiss or anything else, but the way she looked at him there was no mistaking it. She loved him. He couldn't imagine her having anything to do with this, especially now since Evan was gone and she was here. She'd have to wait. He had to get downtown and fast!

Boss Howard got up from the table and went to the phone. "Operator, would you connect me to the office of Stan Peters at the headquarters of the American Red Cross please?" Holding his hand over the mouthpiece he said to Tony, "Get everything loaded up. We're heading out in the morning."

"Stan! Yeah. It's Hal. Say Stan, we are going to have to call off our meeting. Sorry. Yeah I know, but something has come up and I have to leave town. Yeah, but I'll be back as soon as the heat is off. Sure, I'll let you know. Oh, and don't let me down, you know what I mean? Bye Stan." Hall hung up and said to Tony, "I sure hope that light weight Vic can take care of business as well as he thinks he can. If not, I'll lose a lot of dough."

"If he don't," Tony replied, "he'll have wished he did!" The men laughed and went to pack. Little did Hal know that Vic was "taking" care of the business. Skimming- that is…

By the time Andy made it down to the precinct to report in, the snow was piling up and had become a full-fledged blizzard. The news on WCCO said that the city was shut down and traffic was at a standstill. 'Great,' Andy thought. He called the Captain at home and told him the situation.

The Captain said, "Call down to the 15th precinct and let them know what is going on. Maybe they can send over some men before these hoodlums get away! It's all we can
do now."

"But Captain, this is our case, *my case!*" Andy replied.

"I know Malone, but what else have we got? Besides, what's more important, your case or that man?" Malone hung up.

Scully at the front desk had heard the whole of Andy's side of the conversation. He looked at Andy and asked, "What did he say to do?"

"Call the 15th. Will you do it for me right away?"

With a resigned tone Scully said, “Sure Andy, but you know it probably won’t do much good in this kind of weather tonight,” and he placed the call.

Chapter Thirteen- Odd Transportation

Ned had fallen asleep on his bed after he had finished the heavy pasta dinner and vino. He had drunk more in the past two weeks than he had in 20 years! But, this was the best he had felt in four days! His leg didn't even hurt after he had got his cane back. No wonder he had fallen into such a deep sleep. But when Tony came in at five o'clock and woke him up, reality soon hit. He had not heard the guys come into to his room and pack up his things. Things weren't so good. "Get up Ned. We are hitting the road." Ned woke up real quick-like.

Ned looked out the window to see a heavy snow falling on about a foot of new snow on the ground. He called out to Tony, "How are we going to go away? It's a storm out there!"

"Don't you worry about that! The boss has his ways." Ned knew that to be true. In the war Hal had gotten them out of some pretty dire situations over there. He was always one for the unusual- the unpredictable. He was resourceful to say the least. So, Ned knew to expect the unexpected.

Ned got ready and went out to the rest of the group waiting in the front hall of Hal's place. Hal said, "Considering the circumstances, Ned, I'm sending you and Tony on ahead. I was planning on coming along with you, but with this storm I'll have to meet you there."

"Where would that be, Hal?" asked Ned timidly.

"I'm sending you to Florida. I have a place down there where you'll be comfortable and we can still do our business. You know what I mean, Ned?"

Hanging his head he replied, "Sure Hal, I know what you mean." Tony grabbed him by the arm and headed out to the elevator. "But how are we going to get there?" Ned asked again. Tony smiled a big toothy grin and pointed out the window by the elevator. There on the street waited their ride- a city snowplow!

The Sergeant on duty at the 15th precinct took the information from Scully and told him he'd do the best he could. He had three guys out stuck in the snow and two there with him. The rest were all stranded at home. He'd send out the two with him as soon as the sun came up and they could see where they were going. Great! Andy had gotten so close! Once again, he just knew they would get away. Then suddenly at about five- thirty, the snow began to stop. Maybe there would be time! Andy called the 15th again and asked the Sergeant if he would please send the men out now. He came back saying, "Sure Malone, I'll send them right now."

Officers Roller and Salomensen walked up past the Emporium and up to the first of the apartment buildings with a penthouse the Sergeant had told them to investigate. This was tough going! The snow was almost up over their knees. When they turned the corner to go up to the front door, they didn't pay much attention to the snowplow clearing the street, except Roller did find it unusual for there to be three men riding in it. They went up to the door and hit the buzzer to the super's apartment. "Police! Open up! We'd like to ask you some questions," said Roller into the mouthpiece. The door buzzed releasing the lock and they went in.

The superintendent at The Overlook Apartments was also the doorman. Blythe was an Englishman who had at one time served the royal family. When he answered the door, he was preparing to go outside to remove the snow from the walkways. Quite properly, he greeted them saying, "Good day officers, how may I help you?"

Handing him a photograph of Ned, Roller said, "We are looking for this man. His name is Ned. You wouldn't have happened to have seen him in the penthouse would you?"

"The penthouse you say? No, there is a gentleman from Illinois who has the penthouse and he seldom is here. However, I'll ring up to him if you'd like to speak with him yourselves."

"That would be nice," retorted Salomonsen sarcastically.

Tony and Ned got out of the plow no more than five blocks from the penthouse. Five easy blocks compared to having to carry or help an old man with a cane in front of the whole world to the train station. Tony paid for the tickets holding Ned's arm like he was helping him to stand. In reality he didn't want him to try anything—like getting away. It would have been hard to do though, because there weren't many people at the station that morning. He had purchased a whole sleeper car for the two of them! "Nothing too good for the bosses' friends," said Tony to an unappreciative guest.

"The train you will be traveling on will not be delayed sir," said the cashier, "and it is equipped with its own plow just for these conditions. You'll be boarding directly over on track three."

They went out to the tracks and made their way to the train. The steam from an old engine hissed as they passed and the conductor tipped his hat as they approached the stairs of the car. Ned grabbed the handrail and Tony helped him up the stairs to the door of the car. The door was frozen shut. Tony stepped pass Ned and gave it a tug. As he did, Ned looked down and saw the ice on the platform and also saw his chance. He quickly pushed Tony towards the steps on the other side of the car and off he slipped over the side! Ned calmly walked back down the stairs he had just come up and started towards the station house doors. Tony, bleeding over his left eye from the fall, ran to the back of the train and around the caboose. By this time Ned had made his way inside and looked for a place to hide. The conductor was waving his lantern and the train puffed and hissed, and began to move. "All aboard," he shouted and Tony yelled out a profanity. Looking back and forth up the tracks Tony didn't know where Ned had gone. He threw up his hands in desperation. What would the big boss say?

The phone rang and without an answer Blythe hung up. "I'm most sorry officers, but Mr. Howard does not seem to be receiving any calls."

"Then we'll be going up to see this Mr. Howard," said Roller as he made his way to the elevator. Just then the doors of the elevator came open and expecting Boss Howard the two cops drew their guns and positioned themselves so no exit could be made. Out walked a woman and her two poodles, and upon seeing this spectacle, threw up her arms and screamed. In a faint, she fell to the floor. The cops looked at each other and quickly holstered their weapons. They rushed to the woman's' assistance and Blythe grabbed the two dog's leashes. They didn't notice Boss Howard and one of his men slowly descend the back stairs and slip out to his Caddie.

Ned waited in the janitors closet until he was sure Tony had given up and went back to Boss Howard's. It seemed like all day. He'd huddled in fear the whole time. He was such a coward. He'd never been the same since those days in France. The shelling had made him sit in the trenches with his hands covering his ears for what it seemed to be months on end. In fact, it was months! Not until Hal had saved his life when the grenade was tossed in their foxhole had he been able to have a little peace. Since then he had adored Hal. They had been the best of friends until—now. What had happened to Hal? Why so much greed and deception? What did he ever do to him? 'Maybe he felt I owed him,' he thought. "Maybe I do," he said out loud as he snuck out of the closet and out of the train station.

Ned didn't know where to go or who to confide in. He was scared and hungry. It was about four-thirty and the sun was going down. 'All the better. I guess I was in there all day', he thought as he walked toward Ma Klein's. Suddenly out of nowhere a car pulled up next to him, doors flung open, and before you knew it Ned was once again in the back seat of Boss Howard's Caddie.

"Well hello, Ned," said Hal, "nice of you to join us!" Ned looked to the front seat to see Tony with a bandage on his head and an angry snarl on his face.

Ned said to him, "I'm sorry, Tony. No hard feelings?"

Tony just let out a loud, "Humph."

Hal said, "I don't think Tony will make that mistake again." Tony hit the gas and the Caddie roared ahead.

By the time Malone got to the Overlook it was too late. The commotion Roller and Salomonsen had caused was just the icing on the cake. Malone had to try to explain to Peterson why he had let them get away. The hardest part was trying to figure out who they were and where they went. Not to mention how to explain the lady and her dogs!

Chapter Fourteen- A change of scenery

"I've never been somewhere where there wasn't snow at Christmas," said Ned.

Hal laughed and asked, "Do you know where we are?"

"No," Ned replied.

"Good!' shouted Tony from the front seat.

"We must be way down in Florida. I can see both oceans," Ned said.

"That's good enough," said Hal, "this will be a different kind of Christmas. No snow, no shoveling, and no COPS!" The four hoods just laughed. Ned sunk in his seat.

The Caddie glided into the hotel drive and the doorman rushed to open Hal's door even before Tony came to a halt. "Hello, Mr. Howard. Welcome back to the Holiday," he said.

Hal got out and replied, "Thank you, Roberto. I will have an extra guest with me this year. My good friend and associate, Ned."

"Very pleased to meet you, Mr. Ned. I hope your stay with us will be enjoyable."

"Thank you, Roberto," said Ned. They all walked towards the front desk and Roberto and Hals' goons took all the baggage toward the room. Ned's leg hurt from sitting in the car for so long. They had stopped along the way, but only twice at motels to clean up and rest overnight. He clung to his cane and walked slowly with Hal after registering.

Hal pointed to a large house across the road. "Do you see that place over there, Ned? That's Henry Ford's house. He comes down here to get away. Some of those other places are full of rich people, like Hemmingway, this time of year, too. This is the life Ned."

'Hal may have a point,' thought Ned. Ned went straight to his room and got in the tub. He hated to be dirty. It felt great to sit in the warm water and close his eyes. He imagined Suzie and him the last Christmas he had with her. As he lay in the tub he dosed off and dreamed of Suzie.

But then suddenly, a familiar image stood there, Malachi. He said to him, "Ned, God has given you this ability for good- not for evil. Use it wisely. Do not cheat God!"

Slipping in the water he woke with a start. Ned thought, "How in the world could I do that?" He was now accepting the fact that somehow, he was different. Somehow, he *did* have an angel and a gift. He would not let him or God down.

Back in Minnesota, Malone got to work on his hunch about Olga as soon as he got back to the station. He called Tschida's to find out that she had gone home from work already. Then, he called Olga's apartment manager Mr. Harrigan, because Olga did not have a phone to see if she was at her apartment. Fortunately for Malone, Harrigan was home. Unfortunately, Olga was not. "No Officer Malone, she isn't home. Olaf came by and off they went. You know those young love birds nowadays- they just can't spend time apart!"

'Love birds,' Malone thought, 'how could that be if she loved Evan?' He hung up the phone and was even more confused than before. He got up from his chair, put on his coat and headed to Rosie's Bar for lunch. "I'm going to Rosie's'. Anybody want anything?" he shouted before going out the door.

"No thanks, Malone," they all shouted in unison.

Olga just finished her cup of coffee and Olaf paid the check when Malone walked in the door, bell ringing as he closed it tight against the cold draft. "Sure is cold out there, Rosie", Malone said as Rosie stepped up to the counter.

Olga almost spit out the last sip of coffee as she saw who just came in. Containing herself, she slowly got out of her booth as Olaf made his way back from the counter. Malone didn't pay attention to him because he had already turned to go back to hang up his coat by the phone over by the rest rooms.

But Olaf, still happy from his recent good fortune yelled across to Olga, "Come, Olga, let's go buy some Christmas gifts!"

Malone twirled around surprised as to what he heard. What luck! He said, “Say Olga, before you leave can I have a word with you?”

Olaf turned to see who was addressing his future bride. “Hallo, Officer Malone. Tis so nice to see you, for sure,” said Olaf.

“Nice to see you, too, Olaf and you, Olga,” said Andy.

“Vat can ve help you mit Andy?” asked Olaf.

“I’d like to speak with Olga about a recent case concerning an old friend of hers, Evan O’Reilly. Do you know his whereabouts, Olga?”

“Evan O’Reilly? Can’t say that I do, Officer Malone,” replied Olga.

Fidgeting and not wanting to spill the beans about his recent winnings Olaf jumped in, “Oh, I see him at the bowling alley the other day, but not since then, don’t ya know.”

“I thought maybe since Olga and he were good friends that maybe she would know more,” replied Malone.

“Good friends?” Olaf queried, as Olga grabbed him by the arm and led him to the door.

“Sorry we can’t be more help, Andy. Merry Christmas!” yelled Olga as she hastily led Olaf out into the cold afternoon air. Malone raised an eyebrow as he sat at the counter and Rosie handed him a menu. He knew he had to talk with her again.

Meanwhile, Ned came out of his room refreshed from the bath. The warm weather there made it easier for him to walk without his cane. Between that and the booze lately, he wondered why he had never drunk before! He came around the corner into the dining room to find Hal sitting at the table with a paper in his hand. Of course he was reading the sports section.

“Hungry, Ned?” asked Hal.

“Yes, I am,” replied Ned as he sat down to the nicest looking spread he’d ever seen. Fresh fruit, eggs Benedict, bacon, toast- the works! And the view over the tops of the palm trees on the second floor of the hotel was breathtaking.

"This is great, Hal!"

Tony walked up to the table and said, "Boss, there is a phone call from New York and I don't think"…

Hal interrupted him. "Damn! They already know we're here! I'll take it in my room, Tony. Tell them I'll be right there. Enjoy the food, Ned, I'll return shortly."

"Thanks, Hal," replied Ned, almost comfortable in his surroundings knowing he was not really an employee of his good old army buddy, but a prisoner.

Chapter Fifteen- Silent Night- Holy Night!

Sven took the Christmas cookies out of the oven and handed them to Olga. Her oven mitt slopped over the edge and caught one, smashing it. Sven looked at her and she smiled knowing that she would be able to eat it on her break. "Merry Christmas, Olga," said Sven chuckling and smiling back at her.

It was Christmas Eve morning. Sven wanted to make sure he had everything ready for the cases, knowing that this was one of the busiest days of the year. Everyone wanted something special; all different kinds of breads, cookies, and pastry. This time of year he had to be the best baker in town, and he was. But he missed Ned. Next to him, he was second best. And he wondered where he was and what he was doing. Moving to the front of the store with the last tray to put in the case, Sven saw Andy Malone coming down the sidewalk in the snow, his breath puffing out in front of him in the cold. Waving as he came in, Sven greeted him with a cheery "Merry Christmas, Andy!"

"Whew! It's cold out there!" said Malone. "Same to you Sven! Say Sven, I didn't come for pastry today, but I came to speak with Olga if you could spare her for a minute?"

"Ya, sure, ve just finish up. She can take her break now. Olga! Officer Malone is here and he vant to speak mit you," shouted Sven towards the back room. Sven motioned for Andy to go to the back as Olga put down the empty trays on the back room counter. As customers were coming in the front, Thor went to help Sven, and Andy motioned for Olga to follow him to the prep room where they could talk in quiet.

Olga seemed a bit uneasy and Andy knew why. "He doesn't know does he?" Andy asked the unsuspecting Olga.

"Know what?" she replied.

"That you and Evan?" and that was all he had to say for her to break down in tears.

She turned and wiped her face and said, "No he doesn't and he doesn't have to. It would crush him to find out that Evan and I had an affair." Just then, Sven walked into the room and it was too late. Olaf would know. The startled Olga said, "Sven!" But with an ashen look, knowing what he would have to tell his son, Sven turned around and walked back to the front of the store.

"You may as well come clean, Olga! Tell me all you know!"

She proceeded to tell Andy the whole story about the affair, the kidnapping, the sale, and how Evan had always talked about going back home to Belfast. When she was done he asked, "Who's got Ned now and where?"

"I don't know! Some big boss named Hal from Illinois. And I don't know where they took him."

'Another dead end,' he thought. And then the light bulb went off in his head. Illinois!? HAL! Ned's *friend*?

Sven couldn't believe what he had heard. What had Olga done?! He helped a few customers, but couldn't concentrate on what he was doing. After Malone left, Olga came to the front to take over. She looked at him and she saw the hurt in his eyes. As he walked by he said, "Ven da day is over, you not come back."

"But, Sven! Please! Let me talk to you!" she pleaded. He left the room, hand waving behind him to brush her off.

Sven went to the back room and sat down with a cup of coffee. He wondered what Mary would have said. She loved Olaf, but never met him. Sven had met her at the bowling alley one night with her brother Andy. The Sandvigs were wonderful people; proud; honest; hardworking. Sven liked that in a woman. So, he had married her and after a year they were to have a baby. They couldn't wait. But, then there was a problem. And she was gone. Sven had named Olaf all by himself. It seemed odd that they had never picked out names. All he knew is that she would not have wanted to have seen Olaf hurt. And he didn't know how he was going to tell him.

Down in Florida, when he got back to the table, Hal found Ned had already finished and was out on the balcony, sipping his coffee, and looking at the ocean. He followed him out and said, "Ned, I put your first check in the bank for you today."

"My first check?" Ned asked surprised.

"Yes. Your first monthly check of $4,166.66. And, if you do well in your position, you will get a commission."

"A commission on what?" asked Ned.

"Why, your picks of the games of course! If you do as well as I think you can, we can build a good business together you and me, good Buddy." Hal slapped Ned on the back not allowing Ned to say anything about the deal. Ned didn't know what he was in for. Neither did Hal!

About that same time, Malone ran into the station and asked Sgt. Scully to place a call to Chicago and find out who this "Hal" was and what it meant to the case. "I'll get on it right away, Andy," said an excited Scully.

"What's going on?" asked Captain Peterson.

"Well, I think I have a lead on Ned," said Andy, "and it seems that it all points to Illinois, and an old friend named Hal. Do you know anyone in the mob named Hal? Not the kind of name you'd hear in the mob of Chicago is it?"

"One of the vestiges of the "old days" I guess, and after Capone the town was wide open. Maybe the mob let one of the locals work there. Are you finding out about it?"

"You bet, Captain! We're on it!"

"Good work! Let me know what you find out. Merry Christmas everyone! It's time for all of you to go home. Nothing going on here anyhow! The crooks like Christmas, too!"

Across town, the phone rang on the wall at Harrigan's Apartments and he came out of his room to answer it. "Hello, Harrigan's Apartments, Harrigan speaking."

"I would like to speak with Olga Sorenson if I may," asked the caller.

It sounded like long distance to him so he said quickly, "Just a second. I'll see if she's here." Harrigan went to Olga's door and knocked, and speaking loudly asked, "Are you there Olga? The phone is for you?"

Olga answered softly, "I'll be right there, Mr. Harrigan. Thank you." Olga came out to find the phone hanging by the cord in the hall, and Mr. Harrigan gone. The door to Harrigan's room remained ajar, however. Not seeing anyone she picked it up and answered, "This is Olga."

"This is Evan, straight from Belfast, Ireland."

"Evan! Evan!" she almost shouted, "why are you calling me?"

"I just couldn't leave you behind like that me dear, so I called to give you one last chance. I've bought a wee cottage and want you to come here. What say you?"

"Yes, yes, but how?" she asked excitedly jumping up and down.

"I'll have a ticket to New York sent to you and instructions for your passage to Ireland by ship. Look for it by courier today. Merry Christmas, me dear!" The line went dead.

"Evan? Evan?" She rattled the receiver to no avail and hung up. She looked around and saw Harrigan's door close. She knew Evan better send the ticket fast! She quickly went to her room to pack.

The Florida sun began to set slowly over the water and Ned was astounded by the beauty he was seeing. The sun, framed by palms, glowing golden, and like a hot coal extinguished in the water of the bay. He had never seen anything quite like it. In fact, much of his life had been like that lately. First Christmas on the beach for him, too! Ah, Christmas Eve on the beach. What would Suzie think?

Tony called out to him, "Ned it's time to go to church."

"Church?" he replied.

"Yes, church. You're Catholic ain't ya?" Tony asked.

"Yeah," replied the confused Ned.

"Well- get goin then. The boss wants to be there on time."

Hal, despite his flaws, was like all the old timers- if you're Catholic, you go to church on Christmas. Tony pulled the Caddie around to the front and the lights decorating the palms made the glossy black paint on Hal's car dazzle like a thousand stars. "Do you know where we are going Tony?" asked Hal as he and Ned got to the car.

"Yeah, Boss. Division and Eaton. St. Mary's." Tony noticed the cool breeze as he shut the door for Ned. Going around to the other side of the car, something caught Tony's attention from behind the garage on the other side of the street, a BIG limo was beginning to pull out of it toward the street. He wondered who it was. In order for Tony to pull out, he had to wait for the limo driver to pull across and get out of the way. As he watched the car glide slowly past, he observed the window go up ever so slightly to conceal an old familiar face. "Did you see that boss?" shouted Tony.

"What Tony?" asked Hal.

"It was HIM!"

Ned wondered who, "him" was, but looking at Hal's face, he didn't seem concerned. Tony pulled out and went the other direction.

By the time they arrived at St. Mary's, Mass had already begun, but the three of them slipped into the back pew. This was totally different. Ned was struck by all the candles and the images of the Virgin. It was more beautiful than anything he had ever seen before. The mass had begun. "Dominus Vobiscum," said the aging priest.

Picking up the missal, Tony answered without thinking, "Et cum Spiritu tuo."

Soon they went forward for communion. Hal went first, followed by Ned and Tony. Suddenly, as Ned began to kneel, something touched his shoulder. Looking up he expected it to be Tony, but in utter amazement, it was Malachi! Filling the room with light, the crowd looked all around not knowing what to think or from where it came. They could not see what Ned was seeing. Speaking ever so sweetly, the angel proclaimed the Good News of Christmas in Isa. 7:14, "Behold a virgin shall bear a son and they shall call Him Immanuel, God with us." The crowd heard the angel however, and wondered where it was. They all fell to their knees in fear. Ned looked up and saw him. The angel said to him alone, "Fear not Ned, what others have meant to bring harm will come to good." And then, he was gone.

Startled and about to drop the hosts, the priest looked at Ned, who was next to receive the sacrament. He saw the calm look on Ned's face. Coming up to Ned, he reached forward with the host and began to administer it to him, but instead of saying the usual thing he instead said to Ned, "See me after church," and went on.

Tony looked at Ned and shook his head "no" ever so slowly so as no one else would see. The church was aglow with the peace of God. As they left the church, the people were all talking about what had occurred. The priest looked for Ned, but Tony had taken him straight out to the car after communion. Hal didn't know what to think and being scared, he just got in the car and Tony drove off- with no one saying a word. Smiling, Ned just pondered the moment of his first Christmas Eve at the beach!

Chapter Sixteen- Goodbye Olga

Malone had Christmas off, but he didn't want to take it. His wife, Honey, didn't mind, because her parents had come to town and she was able to spend the time with them. They still didn't have any kids. So, Andy went down to the station and asked Scully what he had found out from Chicago headquarters. "Well Andy, there's a mob boss down there called, Hal Howard. It seems he took over just a small part of the town after Capone and the mob couldn't get rid of him. He's been too smart and he's gotten big; mostly into the numbers and rackets. He also has some ties in Florida they said and it looks like here now, too. That's about it though."

"That's our man and that's all I needed Scully. Thanks!"

Over at Harrigan's, a knock came on Olga's door and she looked across the room to see something slide under it. She got up, walked to the door and picked up an envelope. Inside was a ticket for the ten o'clock train to New York City and $500.00 cash! Her eyes got wide and she smiled. Now she knew he loved her. She picked up her bag and made for the door. Down the hall she walked when all of a sudden, Harrigan's door flew open. "Where are you going?" he barked after her.

"Oh, just out of town for a couple of days," said Olga calmly.

"You wouldn't be skipping out on me would you?"

"Oh no, in fact I was going to give you this before I left. I guess I forgot." She produced a twenty and handed it to Harrigan, "That's for January, Merry Christmas!"

"Oh- OK," he said, "thanks." She turned and headed out the door in a big hurry.

At the police station, Malone's phone rang about six times before Andy made it back from the coffee pot to answer it. "Andy Malone," he said out of breath.

"This is Mr. Harrigan. You called me about Olga Sorenson the other day? I don't know if this makes any difference, but she just paid me up front for January and left with a suitcase in her hand. She said something about being out of town for a couple of days."

"I don't know what it means either, Mr. Harrigan, but thanks for the information." He hung up and wondered what Olga had gotten into now.

Ben Egger had just finished dropping off a load at Montgomery Ward on University Avenue and was driving back to the terminal at Yellow Trucking. He wanted to get home to rest after Christmas. There was still a bit of snow on the road from the storm two days before and when the woman stepped out in front of him from behind the bus- it was too late. He just couldn't stop! The big truck jack-knifed and slammed into a light pole before hitting her. When the cops got there they said it was an accident and Egger wasn't at fault. And Olga never made it to Belfast-or the altar.

When Malone heard that news, he called the coroner to see if she had anything on her when she died. "Just a ticket and some cash, Andy," said Jim Cross, rookie coroner.

"Where to, Jim?" asked Malone.

"New York City , and $480.00 cash. That's it, Andy."

"Thanks, Jim." Andy tried to fit that information into the puzzle. Why was she going to New York City ? And where did she get the cash? Andy had some calls to make! And the first was going to be to Stan Peters of the Red Cross.

In Ireland, Evan had just opened the door of his cottage. The phone was not supposed to be hooked up for a couple of days. However, it rang. Evan ran over to the kitchen and picked it up on the fourth ring. "Hallo?" answered the perplexed Irishman.

The voice on the other end said, "She's dead and isn't coming. Fear the Lord." "Click" went the line. Suddenly, the wind began to blow, the window shutters whipped back and forth, and the front door flew open. In fear, Evan dropped the phone. He put his arms in front of him to shield himself from the debris blown by the wind. The roof creaked and a beam cracked sending thatching and wood flying into the room and on top of Evan. His neck was broken. As quickly as the wind had risen, all was now calm.

Ned had slept in after his first midnight Mass in Florida, and it was almost ten o'clock by the time he heard the noise from the street. The patrons of the hotel were all going down to Duval Street to mingle and shop and party, as the town was known to do! A knock came on Ned's bedroom door. "Ned? You awake?" asked Tony.

Rousing, Ned answered, "Yes, Tony. Come in."

"Da Boss wants to see you. He's a little upset about last night."

"Upset about what Tony?"

"Church. He said you never said anything about an angel."

Smiling, Ned answered, "Angel? What Angel?"

Confused, Tony said, "You mean you didn't see no angel last night?"

"Did you?" asked Ned.

"Well, no. Nobody did. Except- it sure looked like you saw something. And the priest thought so, too!"

With a sparkle in his eye Ned said, "Oh, I think a lot of people were caught up in the moment last night. If there was an angel, none of us saw it."

"Well, get ready for lunch. He wants to talk business, too."

"On Christmas?"

"Oh- right. Well, maybe. Just get ready."

Tony related his conversation with Ned to Hal before lunch was ready. "He said there was no angel, huh? Well, I think there was something. I don't know what his game is. But, I'll catch him. My old friend learned everything I ever taught him. So, he knows how to be sneaky!" Hal really didn't know Ned very well anymore and vice-versa.

"Mr. Peter's? This Officer Andy Malone. I would like to speak with you about someone that has come into an investigation in the past few days, a Mr. Hal Howard of Chicago."

"Oh yes, Mr. Howard," replied Stan Peters, "he's one of our largest contributors, especially this time of year. He sponsors the entire Christmas benefit program. He makes it his special contribution to the Red Cross each year. Wonderful man."

Taken aback, Andy responded, "Well, isn't that something? I had no idea."

"Is there anything else I can help you with Officer?"

"Yes, can you tell me if he is in town?"

"As a matter of fact, I spoke with him a couple of days ago and he told me he was leaving, but I don't know to where."

"And ?"

"Yes, Officer?"

"By chance did you know a woman named Olga Sorenson who just was just killed?"

"No, can't say that I do."

"Thanks, Mr. Peters. You've been a big help." Peters hung up the phone and picked it right back up again. He dialed, "0" and heard it connect on the other end. "Operator, get me long distance to Florida please."

Pastor Wenck spoke softly to Olaf as they made their way over to the coroner's to identify Olga's body. "Olaf, I don't know what has happened here with Olga and you, but could you explain it to me?"

Olaf himself had just found out from Sven the conversation he had overheard between Olga and Malone. He was devastated. But now, she was- dead! Jim Cross led them into the morgue. "Oh Pastor! I don't know vat come over her! She was goin off wit anotter man. All da vay to Ireland! She have no family. Just us. Now, I don't have her either."

"We sinners must be forgiving as our Lord is forgiving to us. Perhaps by God's grace she has been forgiven and rests in His arms."

"I sure hope so, Pastor!" Olaf began to cry.

"After this, I'll take care of the arrangements for you Olaf- if you wish?"

"Ya, sure. Dat would be nice of you."

Jim Cross came up to Pastor Wenck and said, "Here are her personal affects. Maybe it can help in some way."

Wenck replied, "Thank you, Jim. And thanks for coming in on Christmas Day."

Pastor Wenck called Martha Wollenberg, the head of the Women's Society, to help with the food and preparations for Olga's funeral. "Sorry to call you on Christmas Day with this Martha, but I needed to talk to you about Olga's funeral."

Martha, as always, was way ahead of him. "Does she have any relatives, Pastor?"

"Not that I know of, Martha."

"Alright. I have everything else all under control. Just make sure you get all the information about her you can over to me before three o'clock, so I can print up the bulletin. I didn't know her very well."

"Will do," responded the cleric. 'Should be an easy one at least,' he thought, 'I've got other things to take care of.'

Chapter Seventeen- Fire!

Hal's phone rang. Tony picked it up and just said, "Talk."

"This is Stan Peters. Is Hal available?"

"Just a second. I'll check," replied the goon. Tony walked into the kitchen and asked Hal, who was sitting with the cook, Diego, while he fixed lunch, if he could come to the phone.

"Who is it?"

"The guy from the Red Cross. That Peters guy."

"Really? Wonder what he wants?" Hal walked out to the phone and answered it. "Yes, Stan?"

"Hal. I had a nosey cop call me about you today."

"Malone?" asked Hal.

"Yes. How did you know?"

"Oh, it just figures."

"Anything to worry about?"

"No, not really, but thanks for letting me know."

"Oh and Hal."

"Yeah?"

"Do you know anything about a girl named Olga? I guess she got killed."

"Olga? Naw. Never heard of her."

"OK. Talk to you later, Hal."

"Thanks, Stan." Ned had been standing in the hall listening to the conversation just when Hal had mentioned Olga.

"Did I hear you mention Olga, Hal?" asked Ned.

"Yeah, someone by that name got killed in St. Paul yesterday. But I don't want you listening to my private conversations, Ned. Got that?"

"Yes, I'm sorry Hal." And Ned walked slowly to the table as lunch was served wondering what had happened to poor Olga. A tear came to his eye and he thought, 'Why Olga, Lord?'

It had taken Pastor Wenck all day long to help Olaf take care of the necessary paperwork downtown. Concordia Lutheran was about five blocks away, and as the cleric drove down Rice Street, he noticed a glow in the early Christmas night sky coming from the direction of the parsonage. He dismissed it as just the sunset. But as he got closer, he noticed a flicker in the window of the church sanctuary and then – BOOM- a huge fireball burst from the stained glass window of Martin Luther and the south side of the building. "Oh Lord!" he exclaimed.

Almost as a reflex action, he hit the brakes and swerved towards the side of the street in the snow. Neighbors came out of their homes after the explosion and getting out of the car he called out to Aleena Bormann, "Aleena! Have your parents called the police?"

"Ya, Pastor. And the fire department, too, for sure!"

Carl felt helpless as he watched the flames grow higher and the building become engulfed in flames that danced like evil demons in a happy conclave. His wife, Jen, came running out of the parsonage, and just walked up and held him, crying. There was nothing else they could do but pray for a new beginning for the fifty year old congregation. The fire trucks from three departments couldn't keep up with the blaze. Besides, by the time they got there it was almost over with anyway. The entire building was a loss. All that was left was the brick sanctuary wall on the North side.

Father McCarthy called Pastor Wenck the next afternoon. "I haven't spoken with my parish as of yet, but if we can be of any service to you and your flock, Carl, please know we are there to support you in any manner."

"As a matter of fact Richard, I have a need right away," Carl said, thrilled with the priests' offer. "Olga Sorensen was killed in an unfortunate accident yesterday. I don't think the facilities at Michotte and Sons will be big enough to handle the entire crowd. May we have the funeral service in your church?"

"That is an unusual request, Carl. You know I will have to call the diocese before I can clear that you know?"

"Do you think it will be a problem?"

"No. But with the tensions of the past it would be wise to see if the diocese agrees this to be a way to bring us closer together."

"God works in mysterious ways, Richard."

"Indeed, my friend. Indeed."

As in WWI, the tensions between the German-American community and the populace were just as strained in this war. Wenck's congregation had a few Scandinavians like Sven and his family, but for the most part, they were comprised of Germans. Even though St. Paul had not had any blatant occurrences of hate crimes, Andy Malone thought he had better check it out in this new investigation. Andy wondered why he had ever offered to volunteer for that special task force. Like he hadn't had enough to do lately! He knocked on the parsonage door and Jen Wenck answered. "Good morning, Officer Malone!"

"My, we are chipper this morning Mrs. Wenck," replied the surprised cop. "I be thinking you'd be down because of the fire?"

"Well yes, Andy, but the Lord will sustain us through this all. Come in out of the cold," and she invited him in.

Carl came out of the kitchen into the living room to greet Andy. "Good Morning Andy, nice to see you again. I expect this is about the fire?"

"Yes, Pastor Wenck. May I call you Carl?"

"Oh yes, Andy, please sit down." Just then the parsonage phone rang.

"Yes, this is Mrs. Wenck. No Captain. I see. May I tell Officer Malone about this? Thank you. Goodbye." Jen turned to address the two men listening to her conversation. "That was Captain Anderson of the fire department. They have investigated the cause of the fire. It was gasoline!" and she began to cry.

Andy's jaw dropped to his chest. Carl got up and comforted his wife.

The sun was up in Florida and Ned had not been able to sleep after hearing the news about Olga. Ned went out to the kitchen and picked up a couple of dirty dishes to put them in the sink. "Oh, no need to do that, Mr. Ned, we take care of everything here," said Diego.

Ned replied, "Oh, I just felt kind of restless and like I haven't done anything for so long. I miss my job."

"What is it you do, Senior?"

"I am a baker, Diego," said Ned proudly in response.

"A baker?"

"Yes, Diego, and a darned good one, too! Have you got an apron I could use? I'd like to whip up one of my specialties."

Enthusiastically, Diego responded, "Si, Senior! I'd like that!"

Back in St. Paul, Father McCarthy called Pastor Wenck as soon as he heard. "I just heard the news Carl. I can't imagine why anyone would want to burn down your building. After hearing the news, Monsignor Durand called me immediately with an enthusiastic "YES" to your request. I'll call Sister Agatha to set it all up for you."

"Thank you so much, Richard. You don't know what this will mean to the family and to the congregation of Concordia."

"Oh, and Carl."

"Yes, Richard?"

"He said you could use it every Sunday night for services if you wish- until you find other accommodations, that is."

"Praise the Lord!" exclaimed Carl. "Thank you all so much!"

Later that day, smells of freshly baked German coffee cake wafted out of the kitchen and throughout the entire bungalow. Hal woke wondering if he was still in Florida. 'What's that I smell?' he said to himself. Tony came in from washing the Caddie. He thought the same thing as he and Hal went straight to the kitchen.

"What are ya doin, Ned?" asked Tony quizzically as he watched Ned putting the finishing touches of drizzled frosting on top of the coffee cake.

"I'm doing what I do, Tony. I bake."

"It sure smells good!"

"And it tastes good, too," said Diego, sampling one of the others Ned had already finished.

Tony walked over and grabbed a bite as well. "HUM? Oh man, this is good!"

Just then Hal came in to join the three men. "What's this? A coffee klatch? Tony get out there and put some wax on that car before it gets too hot. You know what the salt air can do to it. And you, Ned. I don't want you out here fraternizing with the help. You're no longer a baker. You're an investment specialist. Get out of that apron and come out on the veranda." Hal walked out and Ned looked at Tony and Diego. Not saying a thing, Ned took off the apron in disgust and threw it on the prep table, flour flying all over the kitchen.

Things were going better in Minnesota and fortunately for Martha, when she got done with the bulletin at the church, she took them home with her to fold before the funeral. They were a lot of work and a labor of love. She had been the last one in the church before the fire. Martha had left about three-thirty PM and had not noticed anything unusual before she did. That's what she told Officer Malone when he called her. "Yes officer, everything was just as normal. No one else had even come in all day. I was all alone and not much happens on Christmas Day."

As Andy didn't get much information from Martha, he went to talk to some of the neighbors. Mrs. Frattalone only had one thing to say. "Oh, I did notice one thing though, not that it matters, but the fuel oil guy came to fill the tank about two o'clock."

"Which company do they use?"

"Katz Brothers."

“Thank you Bonita, you’ve been a lot of help,” said a thankful Malone.

On the contrary for Ned, Hal was not being a help in Florida. Ned came out to the veranda hot as a three dollar pistol. “Before you say anything Ned,” remarked Hal when he stepped outside, “I want you to think about your circumstances. In all actuality, you are mine. Like an asset about to be used like any other. But, I’ve offered you a better life and a job that can make you a wealthy man. If you want to bake the rest of your life…” Suddenly, comically, and without warning a huge pelican flew over Hal dropping a fish on his head! “Oh crap!” shouted Hal as he shook off the fish and raced to the bathroom to clean off the mess.

Ned broke out in spontaneous laughter at the sight and Diego rushed in to help the smelly, crazed Hal. Ned looked up to the sky and whispered, “Thanks.”

Chapter Eighteen- Funeral One- Olga

St. Bernard's sanctuary had seating for five-hundred in the pews. If they filled the narthex with chairs and opened the doors they could get another hundred or so in there. And that's what they had to do. It seemed like everyone wanted to see all about this girl that no one knew. All the Catholics were there and all the Lutherans, too, as well as the press to cover the story of Olga, Concordia's burned church, and the relationships between the two congregations. Except for the war, it was the local story of the year. In the sacristy, Pastor Wenck and Father McCarthy discussed the situation. "I wish this many of my people came to Mass on a regular basis."

"Don't ya know, me too," said Carl, "I guess we're all together today. But how do we stay that way?"

"The love of God," said Richard.

Carl signaled the organist to begin the first hymn. After it was over, he stood to welcome the mourners. "Dear brothers and sisters in the Lord. Today we come together to mourn the loss of a child of God. Let us pray."

Timothy Flanders spoke softly as Wenck faced the altar to pray. "I'm not their brother. Since when do we pray with German Lutherans?"

"This is just a funeral, Tim. Now be quiet and have some respect!" said Mathew Donahue. Even though they were trying to be quiet, Andy Malone heard them three rows back. It was enough for him to know just how tense it was on Rice Street and to know how far relations had to go.

After the funeral, the crowd filed into the cafeteria for the food the women of both congregations put together. Martha came up to Pastor Wenck as soon as he got disrobed and came across the alley. "Pastor, I have to say that the women here have been just wonderful! I am so impressed on how hospitable they have been."

"That is indeed a prayer answered," replied Carl and he went to the head of the table to say the blessing. As he turned, he saw them all take off their hats and bow their heads. "Lord, amidst the trials of war, the strife of conflict, and the realization that death comes to all us sinners, and as we celebrate the life of Olga this day, let us remember the good, and recall those special things we hold dear. Now bless this food, the hands of those that have prepared it and those that share their blessings with us, always knowing it all comes from you. In the name of Jesus our Savior."

"Amen," resounded the congregations. After the prayer, they all fell into line and started to eat.

Father McCarthy came up to Andy Malone in the back of the room. He was watching the crowd to see if there was any inclination of a problem. To his delight it didn't seem like it would be so, at least today. "Watching all my boys are you Malone?" asked the priest.

"Yes, Father, you know I am."

"Well, as long as there's food things will be fine. Why don't you relax and get a plate for yourself?"

"I think I will, Father," and winking at him, the cop stepped to the rear.

Martha sat down next to George, her husband, who was already eating. Not wanting to sit next to any of his possible suspects, Andy sat across from Martha in the only chair available. "Hello, Mrs. Wollenberg, may sit across from you?" asked the polite cop.

"Why yes, Officer Malone. This is George, my husband."

"Very nice to meet you, Mr. Wollenberg," said Andy. George stuck out his hand and just shook Andy's as he had just put a fork full of food into his mouth. Sitting down, Andy noticed George's jacket with the embroidered pocket. It said "Katz Bros." on it. "Oh George, I see you work for Katz Brothers. I didn't know that."

Martha piped in, "Oh yes, he's worked there for thirty-five years now. He's almost about to retire."

"You never mentioned that the other day."

"Why, I never thought about it. Why would that be important? I mean, George just stays in the office and never comes out to fill the tanks. It was one of the men on the crew that filled the tank the other day."

"Yes, I guess so. It's not important." George smiled and just went on eating and never said a word.

When Andy got back to the station, he sat down and wrote a list of all the things that had occurred in the past fortnight. Scully came up to his desk and sat down. "Say Andy, I think I got a lead on the location of Hal Howard. He has a place in Florida in the Keys. It's right across the street from Henry Ford's place!"

"Really? Upscale kind of guy this, Hal Howard. I wonder how a guy with the name "Howard" got involved with the Italians? Have you called the cops in Miami about him?"

"Yeah, but they aren't cooperating. If you know what I mean."

"Yeah, unfortunately, I do. That means if anything is going to happen, I'll have to contact the FBI and I don't want to do that. They'll take this case from me in a heartbeat. Or, I can go there myself. What's the chance in the boss letting me do that?"

Scully got up and laughed, "About one in a million I guess, Andy!"

"I guess I have no choice then do I?" Andy picked up the phone.

Ned was sitting reading the paper and listening to the news. The sound of the surf and the gulls was about to put him to sleep in the warm ocean breeze. Then he heard it. "This afternoon the FBI took on the case of a missing baker from Minnesota. Abducted two weeks ago, the man, Ned Oelker, was last seen in a black Cadillac from Illinois heading toward the Florida Keys. It is presumed the men who abducted him are armed and dangerous. If anyone has any information concerning…" The radio went silent. Tony had shut it off. "Don't get any ideas Ned. It won't do any good."

"Great! Just great! If I didn't have bad luck, I'd have no luck at all!" Hal threw his Cuban cigar out the window.

"I guess we'll just have to move again, huh, boss?" asked Tony.

"That's where you get yourself into trouble all the time Tony. Trying to do the thinking for me. Yes, we're going to move, but not to where they think. Get Ned ready before the FBI has a chance to catch up with us. Besides the Godfather knows where we are and I don't trust him. Our vacation is over."

"Aw, Boss," Tony protested, "I wanted to go to Sloppy Joes tonight!"

After making his call, Andy set aside his involvement with Ned's disappearance for the time being and concentrated on the fire at Concordia. 'What's the connection with George Wollenberg?' he thought to himself. 'Why would the husband of one of the members try to burn down the church? Or did he have anything to do with it at all?' It was still all a mystery to him.

Andy's phone rang. "Malone," he answered.

"This is Sam Goodhall of the FBI. I thought I'd let you know that we followed up on your lead to the residence of Hal Howard in Key West. Sorry to inform you that by the time we got there he had already left."

"You mean he was there and you missed him?"

"What do you mean by that?"

"Nothing at all, Sam. I just can't believe it! They got away again! Have any idea which way they went?"

"No trace."

"Thanks for the call, Sam." Andy hung up the phone. "Rats!"

Chapter Nineteen- Malachi Appears

Ned was asleep when Tony stopped the car to fill up the tank at a Texaco and stretch his legs. Hal got out and came around the back. "I think we gave them the slip Boss." Tony said. Hal lit up a cigar. He puffed a couple of times and the tip burnt bright red. Tony laughed and said, "I think you better move back boss or the back of this Caddie is going to take off like a rocket!"

"Don't worry Tony, I won't blow us up, but the Godfather would like it! But, I think you're right. They have no idea we're going back to the Twin Cities and they won't be expecting it either."

Ned had woke up just long enough to overhear the plan and kept his eyes closed. 'Good, I'll be home for the New Year! 1945!' he thought to himself.

At about the same time, Andy paid a visit to Capt. Anderson at fire station number three. "Have you got any more information on the fire at Concordia, Captain?"

"As a matter of fact, the results of the examiner came in this morning. The accelerant wasn't gasoline after all. It was a form of jet fighter fuel. There isn't much of it around here and it would have had to be someone with the ability to appropriate it."

"Why would anyone use it?" asked Andy.

"Well, when ignited, it burns fast and hot. If you wanted to get something going and not have to worry, this is the trick."

"Tell me Captain, could a fuel oil company get it?"

"Sure, they can buy anything as long as there is a demand."

"Thanks for the update, Captain."

"You bet, Andy."

About ten minutes later, George Wollenberg came in from the yard to his office to find Andy waiting for him. He was taken aback. "Well hello, Officer? I'm sorry I've forgotten your name."

"Officer Andy Malone."

"That's right, Malone. What can I do for you, Malone?"

"I'd like to inquire about a certain fuel and see if you have any customers that use it, George."

"What would that be, Andy?"

"Jet fighter fuel."

"Well, we did have a new prototype fuel come in that we were supposed to sell to the government, but only five gallons came in for testing in our lab. Why?"

"Where would it be now?"

"I don't know Malone, but I'm sure it's out there."

"Let's go see."

"Do you have a warrant?"

"Do I need one or are you going to cooperate with this investigation?"

"I'll cooperate, but I don't see what this has to do with a church fire!"

"I didn't say it did," responded Andy.

George led him out to the fuels shed. When he got to the door, there was a bar leaning there that was used for closing the door at night. As George walked by, he picked it up and turned to face Andy. "You know it's not here Malone. I'm not going to let you take me in either!" With that, he swung the bar with such force that when it hit Andy it shattered his arm like a twig. He winced in pain and as he grabbed it, Wollenberg grabbed for his gun. Andy got it out first and they struggled. BANG! The gun went off striking George right between the eyes. Hearing the shot, Bruce Katz ran out to find both men lying on the floor. Andy was unconscious. George was dead.

When Andy woke, he was at Midway Hospital. A nurse was checking his pulse. "Oh," he said as he felt the first twang of pain from his arm.

"Sorry, Andy. I'll be giving you a little bit more to kill the pain. The fella you ran into shattered your arm. It's going to take a long time to heal," said the nurse as she adjusted the height of his bed and left the room.

Just then, Duke Ellington began to play on the radio somewhere. Andy looked around. He could not tell where it was coming from. The nurse came back into the room, hypodermic needle in hand. "Roll over Officer, I have only one place I can apply this."

Knowing what she meant he said, "Oh," and rolled over. Trying to take the tension from the situation he asked, "Where is the music coming from?"

"Mr. Stan Peters from the Red Cross brings a radio in for the service men in the community center. He comes almost every day. Such a nice man."

'Stan Peters, huh?' he thought to himself. It wasn't long before the shot took effect and Andy was out for the night. About three am, he woke when someone came in the room and walked into the tray table to the left of his bed. Startled, the person ran off out the door. Andy shouted out the best he could in his drugged condition, "Nurse! Nurse!" He fell back to sleep and never knew if the nurse came or not.

Capt. Peterson was at Andy's bed the next morning when he woke. "Capt. Is that you?"

"Who else did you think it was?" replied the tough, old cop.

"Oh, I don't know. Someone was I my room last night. It was probably just a nurse."

"Yeah. Say Andy, you want to tell me what happened at Katz Brothers the other day?"

"Yeah. Well, I got a funny feeling when we were going out to the storage shed that he was going to pull something on me and he did. How long did the Doc say I was going to be out?"

"About six months."

"Six months?!" said the startled cop.

"Yeah, and there's nothing you can do about it. It's either that, or lose the arm. You want that?"

"No, but what *can* I do?"

"I'll put you on detail in the office. You can follow up on all the loose ends for the detectives working on these open cases. All I know is that's better than sitting at home with the missus!"

Pastor Wenck addressed the assembly in front of the burned out hull of Concordia. It was very cold and with each word his breath accentuated his speech. It was just about sun down and the atmosphere surreal, "Dear friends. As many of you know the church was under-insured. By the providence of God, we no longer had a mortgage. However, because of this, we now need fifty-thousand dollars to rebuild and serve this community. Let's bow our heads, give thanks to God, and seek His will."

As he turned to face the charred remains of the once grand building, a white light began to replace the sun. It was indiscernible at first and no one noticed. But as it grew, pulsating in hues of green and blue, the people no longer paid attention to Pastor Wenck in his prayer and instead focused their attention to what seemed to be an image on the only wall left standing; the north wall. Someone said, "Look, it's the northern lights."

However, the light grew more distinct taking on the form of a being. A little girl in the front said pointing for her mother, "Look mommy, an angel!" Indeed it was an angel, Ned's angel, Malachi!

"People of the Lord Jesus at Concordia," he began, "do not be discouraged. From your community, God shall provide."

In awe, some fell to their knees. A woman in front proclaimed, "Praise be to God!" And then, Malachi was gone.

Pastor Wenck raised his voice above the crowd and said, "God has answered our prayers friends. Go home and tell the world about what happened here tonight!" Slowly and still in shock, the crowd dispersed, giving God the glory.

Chapter Twenty- Watch out Malone!

It was almost New Years Eve. Tony drove to the back entrance of The Overlook where he and Ned had boarded the snow plow just a few days earlier. The revelers in the banquet hall provided all the cover they needed to make their way up the back stairs and to the elevator on the fifth floor. This private party was for some of the wealthiest people in town. It was usually attended by Hal. He felt bad he couldn't go. The more connections the better in his line of business! But it was not to be.

Tony drove the Caddie over to a storage unit by the river and Hal picked up the phone to call him a cab right after he and Ned got into the penthouse. "That's right. Right by the Schmidt Brewery. He'll be there waiting."

Hal knocked on Ned's door. "Say Ned, I think I'd like to see if you'd pick a winner for me tonight. It's time for the last hockey game of the year. The St. Paul Saints play." Ned frowned. "Come on, I haven't asked you to do it before. Humor me."

Ned said, "What time is it? I miss my watch!"

"It's six-fifty."

"Alright. It'll be 3-0 Saints."

"Goodnight, Ned," said Hal and he gently shut the door.

Ned went to his nightstand and picked up a Bible in the drawer and lay down. It was a Bible the Gideons had placed there. He flopped open the book and it fell to the prophet Malachi. "That's funny," Ned said to himself. There on the top of the page was the third chapter, verse eight. "Will a man rob God? Yet you are robbing me! But you say, "How have we robbed thee?" Ned fell asleep.

Hal placed the bet with just two minutes to spare. He tuned in on KSTP and listened to the entire game. He found it was more exciting this way; not that he hadn't ever placed a bet on a game before! Ha! That was not it. It was because he wanted to see if Ned was right. He wanted to see if this was real. He wanted to see—if he was going to be a rich man! Sure enough after all of the excitement, Ned was- right. The Saints won 3-0. It was the most exciting game Hal had ever listened to. He was sure it would not be his last. He called Vic to see what he won. "They had them down by four, Boss. You won seven grand."

"Thanks, Vic," replied a delighted Hal.

When Ned woke up the next morning, the doorman had already put the Pioneer Press inside the room door. His eye caught the headline for the local section before the main page because it was a big surprise for him. "Angel appears to Lutherans after fire." 'What?' thought Ned, 'It can't be!' He tore off the front couple of sections and found the Local Section front page. On it was a picture of the burned out shell of Concordia with an image of an angel, or what looked like an angel to some. The reporter interviewed parishioners who told the story of how they heard the angel and what it said. Remembering what he had read the night before, "Oh my, I know what I have to do," said Ned to himself.

Andy wasn't too happy he was in the hospital for New Years Eve. All the help was let off except for a skeleton crew. The patients were bedded down for the night and the place was, almost dead, so to speak. He waited for the nurse to come past his room. She put her head in and asked, "Anything I can get you before I tend the desk? I'm here alone for the night now."

"Yes! Some company!"

"Well, sorry I can't help you with that. But if you get me your home number, I'll let you talk to your wife at midnight on the phone."

"That would be great!" That made the cop one happy man until the lights....

Betty Rippentrop had married the nephew of the famous Nazi, Joachim Von Ribbentrop. She remembered the whole thing and as she went to work it raced through her mind once more...

Gerhard was second generation German American, and the people knew he was a loyal American citizen. There were never any problems until Wollenberg had called. "I have an order here for you for four pallets of concrete block and two tanks of propane

Gerhard. And Gerhard, have you thought about the proposal I spoke to you about last week?"

"Ya, George. But I can't do that! They, no, I won't," replied the mason.

"Alright, Gerhard. But time is running out. If you don't, you know the consequences."

Gerhard hung up the phone. He told Betty the whole thing. Wollenberg knew Gerhard gambled and owed Vic money, so somehow he thought he had something on Gerhard and now that the war was wrapping up and tensions were high, he was blackmailing Gerhard. Gerhard didn't fall for it. "What does he want you to do?" asked Betty.

"He wants me to burn down Concordia Lutheran Church."

"What? Why would he want you to do that?" replied an astonished Betty.

"I don't know. He never said."

Betty came up the service entrance to the penthouse and hung her coat in the butler's pantry. She had not been there for a long time. She had not come in before the holidays because Boss Hal had left so quickly. She didn't think anything of that because, well, that was just how the boss was. She had not stocked the kitchen in a long time. But for some reason when Tony called her, he said that the boss wanted it stocked for a long period of time. No problem, but it would be hard to get some things, like sugar and coffee. "The war will be over soon and things will get back to normal," she said to herself. But Hal had ways to get even the hardest things to find. He would just have them delivered. She never asked questions. Maybe that's why she still had her job. Ned came out to the kitchen. "Hello, my name is Ned."

"Hallo, I am Betty."

"Nice to meet you. Do you have anything in the kitchen for baking?" inquired the bored baker.

"Well, yes I do, but there are some things in short supply until I stock the kitchen. But, *I* usually do all the cooking," she said.

"Oh, I sometimes get bored," replied Ned, "and I like to throw something together from time to time."

Protective of her space, Betty remarked, "Well, I don't like people in my kitchen, but if the boss says it's OK."

Knowing how the boss would respond to that, "Great", whispered Ned under his breath and he walked back into the dining room. As the door swung back and forth Betty said, "I'll put on some tea."

The lights to the east wing of Midway Hospital flickered off. It was eleven-thirty pm. While waiting for his phone call, Andy had been reading and was sitting up in his bed with his cast propped on his lap. His door was cracked open a bit and he looked out. He saw and heard nothing. He was suspicious, so he got up straining under the weight of his arm cast which was bent at an angle. He stood by the door. Slowly it began to move. He was about to raise his cast to use it as a weapon when he heard a voice, "Andy? Are you there?"

Recognizing the voice he replied, "Honey? Is that you?" He breathed a sigh of relief as she stepped through the door. They pushed the door open so the light from the west wing could filter into the room. Still, they couldn't see much. The door across the hall came open and thinking it was the nurse Andy said, "Say nurse, do you have any candles?" But it wasn't the nurse. The figure took one step toward him and fired a shot that passed his head and lodged in the wall. Andy pushed Honey to the floor. A second shot rang out, this one hitting his cast. Andy picked up the closest thing to him, a bedpan, and flung it toward the figure catching it square in the face. It rang out like a bell, but the figure just ran toward the west wing and disappeared.

Heads began popping out of rooms and the nurse came in saying, "Is everybody all right in here?"

"Yes we are," replied Malone.

Picking Honey off the floor she asked, "What was that all about, Andy?"

"I don't know Honey, but I'm going to find out!" Just then, in rooms throughout the building people were shouting, "Happy New Year!!!" He pulled Honey closer and gave her a kiss.

A little later, Captain Peterson came in the room with a piece of party confetti hanging off his ear. "What's going on here, Malone?" snapped the testy veteran.

"It looks like somebody wants me dead, Captain," said the calm Malone. "What I can't figure out is- why?"

"You obviously got under somebody's skin. Think Malone, think. Who's toes have you stepped on lately?"

"I don't know Captain, but it looks like I must be doing my job, huh?"

"Yeah, Malone. Don't get too cocky! You got me out of a party! Well, I guess it was time to go anyway." He brushed the confetti off his head. "Glad you're OK. You too, Honey. Think about this and let me know tomorrow. I'll stop by."

Honey looked at Andy and smiled. "I'm staying the night, Andy. If you promise I won't get shot at again!"

"Don't worry, Dear, no one is that stupid."

Chapter Twenty-One- Pennies from heaven!

Blood ran down her face as she cleaned the wound in the mirror. How was she ever going to go out looking like this? She'd have to lay low until it healed enough. But how? She was in charge of the meeting on Thursday night! Maybe she could come up with an excuse. That stupid cop, Malone! Next time, she'd get him- for sure!

Spent from the emotional evening, Pastor Wenck sat and opened the mail when he came home from the rally. It had been a long day and the mail had fallen through the slot into a box he left under it in the coat closet. On the bottom of the pile was a bulging envelope with no return address. Postmarked from St. Paul, it was addressed to Concordia in care of him, which was not unusual. But this was not a business envelope and he could tell it was written by an older person; shaky handwriting. Opening it without care, he found a piece of paper folded three times and inside, $4,650.00 in cash! He looked again in the envelope to see if there was a letter. Scribbled there was only this, "Monthly offering." He said to himself, "God truly answers prayer!"

Ned called Tony to the table. "Say Tony, if I wanted to go shopping would that be possible?"

Tony answered politely and said, "Not necessary, Ned. Just tell me what you need and I'll be happy to take care of it for you. That's my job."

"Oh," Ned answered disappointingly. "I need some new shoes and a suit. If I'm going to work for Hal, I have to look the part."

Perking up excitedly Tony replied, "Yes sir! I'll get everything you need!" Tony went into see Hal as soon as he was finished getting the information from Ned. "Boss, I just got to tell you,"— but Hal cut him off so he could finish up on the phone.

He hung up. "Yes, Tony?"

"Boss, Ned just told me to go get him a suit! Said if he was gonna work for you, he had to look the part!"

"Well I'll be!" said the baffled Hal.

Meanwhile, Pastor Wenck answered the phone, "Concordia Lutheran Church."

"Pastor Wenck, this is Officer Andy Malone. I hate to have to tell you this, but as they were cleaning out the basement of the church, the crew found a body."

"Dear Lord!" exclaimed the minister. "Do you know who, but why, and where, oh my! What does this mean?"

"I don't know," replied Andy, "but I'm going to find out. When the coroner gets done, I'll let you know what we have."

"Thank you, Andy. I'll have to inform the congregation."

"I be asking you to wait on that, Pastor. We may be able to find out more that way."

"OK, Andy. I'll trust you to be up front with me so I can be with my congregation."

"Don't worry, Pastor. And thanks!"

In the Sunshine State, Hal walked up to Ned as he tried on the suit coat Tony had picked out for him. "Do you like it? It's Italian."

Laughing, Ned replied, "What else would it be?"

"Yeah," said Hal, "Ned, I need to have you do me a favor. Could you pick the winner of the next horse race in California?"

"To tell you the truth Hal, I don't know."

Getting a little bit testy Hal said, "What do you mean?"

"Well, I've never tried that before and it isn't a real *game*. I guess I could try."

"OK, I'll get the card and we'll see. Thanks."

"Don't mention it."

Hal was surprised by Ned's reaction and wondered what all this "cooperation" was all about.

Meanwhile, Martha walked into the church office in the parsonage just after Pastor Wenck hung up the phone. Raising his head and smiling, he looked at Martha and said, "That's a lovely scarf you have there Martha, I didn't know you wore them."

"Well, George got it for me for Christmas and I don't have a black hat. I thought I'd come by to see how the arrangements were coming for his funeral and if someone else could fill in for me for a while in the office."

Coming over to her to give her a hug, Wenck was surprised when Martha withdrew. "Are you alright, Martha? I know this is hard for you. But tell me what could have prompted this kind of behavior from George?"

"I don't know Pastor. I just don't know." She began to weep.

Then- he saw it. A big gash on her forehead almost behind her hairline! But he didn't say anything. Instead he offered her a chair and responded to her question about the funeral. "Here Martha, sit down. The funeral is set for Saturday at two PM. I have a couple coming in for premarital counseling in the morning. As we don't have a building, and we won't be expecting as many people as Olga's funeral, I guess we'll have to do it at Michoetti's. Jen will take care of all the arrangements and she has offered to fill in for you until you feel up to coming back."

"Thank you so much, Pastor!"

"I hope that in all of this you are reassured of God's love and His grace." Turning away, she cried some more and walked out the door.

Ned looked out the window of the penthouse knowing that in reality he was a prisoner, but playing along with the part that Hal had concocted. The lights in the park reflected off the snow that had been falling all day long. They were small flakes in the cold winter day, blowing, swirling, and dancing along the trees and glistening in the moonlight as it settled down. Now, every one of them shone like stars under the light. He saw a man walking his dog, his breath billowing out from under his scarf. The dog was not waiting for him and pulled him quickly toward the center of the park. Hal interrupted his minds' wanderings with a question as he entered the room. "Are you ready?"

"For what?" Ned inquired.

"To pick a winner!"

"Oh, that. Sure, let's give it a try."

Hal handed the paper to Ned. He looked at the times and the horses that were about to run. "This one starts in ten minutes in India! I'll try to do it, but usually, it has to be a "game" you know. You can't place a bet on a horse after the race has started can you?"

"No," said Hal, "just try it."

"OK, but I don't know. It just doesn't feel right." With that he circled the three top horses in each race and handed it back to Hal. "I wouldn't bet the farm on them, Hal," Ned said.

"I'll be careful. Thanks."

Hal left the room and Ned just sighed and looked out the window again. He saw a car pull up to the front entrance. A man with a beard got out and opened the door for the occupant in the back. Out stepped the most beautiful woman he had ever seen. He tried to follow her as she made her way in, but lost her from view. Ned wondered who she could be.

Chapter Twenty-Two – Funeral Two-Martha Moves

"Officer Malone?" asked the woman at the counter.

Andy had gone to Schneider's Grocery to pick up some chicken for dinner on the way home. "Yes, I'm Malone", he answered.

"I heard you were in charge of the investigation at Concordia Lutheran. Could I speak with you outside?"

When the two of them were finished being checked out, they walked out past the front doors into the cart area where it was protected from the outside wind. "I'm Betty Rippentrop. My husband Gerhard, he has gone off for days before, only because of his drinking, but he's always come back. He's never very busy in the winter, but he's been gone three days now. The last thing before he left, and the reason I'm speaking to you is that, he spoke to George Wollenberg on the phone. He was so upset." Lying she added, "But he didn't tell me what it was about. I don't know what to do."

Andy got visibly excited. "Thank you for the information, Betty. I think I know where your husband is. I'm going to call my wife and tell her I'll be late. Lets' go down to the station."

When they got to his desk and Betty was sitting down, he explained the situation with the body in the basement of Concordia. She broke down. "We'll need to go to the coroner and have you identify his body." Through the tears she nodded in the affirmative.

Getting up, Malone was stopped by Scully. He whispered in his ear, "I've seen this one before and I think she works for some of the undesirables."

"OK, Scully, thanks," he whispered back. They put on their coats and walked slowly toward the basement and the coroner.

"What if you are wrong and it's not Gerhard?" she asked as her voice echoed down the hall.

"Then I keep looking."

As they entered the cold offices the coroner, Jim Cross, came up to them. "How can I help you, Andy?"

"We'd like to see the body that came in from Concordia. This is Betty Rippentrop, Jim."

"Pleased to make your acquaintance. It's right over here." Jim pulled out the drawer and began to pull back the sheet. It stuck to the burned flesh and he had to tug on it. When he did the stench was foul. Betty almost lost it, but turning to the side and then looking back, was able to continue. She had to look closely for a moment. She started to sob and nodded yes. Then, she walked out of the room. "That's Gerhard Rippentrop, Jim. Now all we have to do is find out why and who did it."

When Andy and Betty left, Jim Cross picked up the phone and dialed his friend, Matt Stein, at the Pioneer Press. "Hey Matt. Have I got a story for you! But it'll cost ya fifty bucks. OK. Ya know that stiff that came in from the Concordia fire?"

Betty waited for Andy in the hall. "It was that evil George Wollenberg! I don't know what he said to him that night on the phone, but it had to have been him. I just know it!"

"The evidence seems to point that way, but we'll have to look at all the clues before we make a determination. I'd hate to see someone get off Scott- free."

"Maybe you're right. We don't want to jump to conclusions. But, who?"

"I'll find out for sure. Don't worry. Are you going to be alright?" She nodded, yes. "Thanks for coming in." Betty walked out the front door and Andy went to his desk and called Pastor Wenck.

He answered on the fourth ring. Andy said, "Pastor, this is Andy Malone. I think you better get ready for another funeral."

"What?" replied the surprised clergyman.

"It's Gerhard Rippentrop."

Tony sat the newspaper in front of Ned and walked to the coffee pot to pour them each another cup. The headlines read, "Body found in basement of Concordia Lutheran!" Ned picked it up and read the article. 'I know that guy, in fact, isn't that Betty's husband?' he said to himself. He quickly folded the page over and began to read another page. As he brought over the coffee and sat down at the table, Tony motioned for him to pass the paper to him. Ned picked up the other sections and handed them to Tony, and continued to read the section he had.

Hal walked in. "Good morning, guys. How did we do on the ponies?"

Tony opened the sports and looked at the race results. "Not so good, Boss. In fact, we didn't win a thing."

"See. I told you," Ned chimed in, """it" doesn't work unless it's a *game*."

"I see that!" exclaimed Hal, "And I took your advice. I only bet five bucks on each race. Still, I lost two-hundred bucks."

"So now we know not to do that again," said Tony.

"Right. So today we bet on basketball." Hal took a cup of coffee. Just then, Betty walked in with the sack of groceries she had bought the night before.

"Hello, Betty", said Tony to her.

She was not herself and he could tell when she answered, "Hallo."

Hal left the room to go sit in his chair by the window and drink his coffee. Betty started to put away the things.

Tony got up and went out to start the car and said, "I gotta do some stuff for da boss. I'll be back soon."

Ned waited until he left and saw his opportunity. "Say Betty," he inquired, "I saw the article about Gerhard." She turned and as soon as their eyes met she began to cry and walked over to Ned and put her arms around him! Taken aback by this sudden show of emotion, Ned held her at bay, but to no avail. Sensing his discomfort, she backed off a little and said, “I better get going. I need to see Pastor Wenck about the arrangements.”

“My sympathies, Betty.”

“Thanks, Ned. See you in a few days.”

Meanwhile, Martha quickly walked home. She knew Pastor had seen it. After she went in, she took off the scarf and walked to the mirror. AH! She got out her makeup and started to cover the gash again, but it was deep enough and it was still visible. Then she got an idea, the wig! She went to the closet and pulled out a wig she had used in a play at church. It matched her hair well and she pulled it down far enough to cover up the wound. It did look out of place that far down onto her face, but with the scarf, she could make it work until after the funeral, and then- she was taking it on-the-lam. She had relatives in Nova Scotia and no one would find her there! Now that the body had been found, she knew her time was up in Minnesota. That stupid cop Malone was starting to get too close!

Andy Malone knocked on the parsonage door. Jen opened it and said, “Please come in Officer. I’ll see if Carl has anyone in the office.” Leaving him sitting on the couch, she went to the rear of the house and Wenck’s office.

“Please come back here, Andy,” yelled Carl from his office. Andy got up and then he saw it- a picture of Carl, Jen, George, Martha, Betty, Gerhard, and another man and his wife hanging on the wall in the hall. He stopped to look at it. Carl said, “Isn’t that a great picture? We were at a retreat up North. Nice cabins, lake, and the fishing was great.”

“I know most of the people in it, but who’s this couple here?”

“Oh, that’s Stan Peters and his wife Marge. They aren’t members, but the Red Cross sponsored the event. He’s a nice man.”

“So they say,” remarked Andy and he followed him down the hall to the office.

Once in, Carl closed the door. “What can I do for you today, Andy? Is there more news on the fire?”

"No Pastor, but I'd like to ask you about Martha Wollenberg."

"You missed her by about an hour, Andy. She was in to discuss the arrangements for her husbands' funeral. It's set for Saturday."

"Does she have family here?"

"No, and I don't know where she is from. She and George had only been married for a few years and even though I saw her three days a week in the office, we never talked about her past. They had no children and they kept to themselves, but she was efficient and did her job with pride and to the glory of God. And I'm worried about her. She must have bumped her head or something because she had a big gash on her forehead."

Malone got excited, but didn't let Carl know. "Really? I see. Is she staying on as your secretary?"

"Well, she is going to take a leave of absence for a month, but I assume it is because of this whole affair."

Just then, someone rang the doorbell. They could hear Jen answer it and head back to the office. She knocked and said, "Carl, its Betty Rippentrop to see you."

"I'll be just a couple more minutes dear."

"Is that about all Andy?"

"Yes, Pastor and thanks. I'll be going to see Martha as soon as I can."

"Let me know if there's anything more I can do."

Andy walked out to the parlor and tipped his hat to Betty and said, "Mrs. Rippentrop, I'd like to call on you to get a little information about Gerhard. May I come by, say, nine o'clock tomorrow morning?"

"Sure, Officer. I got nothing to hide. See you tomorrow." She walked down the hall and he walked out the door. He walked quickly to the office. Now he knew- Martha had tried to kill him!

The chapel at Michoetti's was full when Andy arrived. 'Good, I can sit in the back,' he thought. Behind him he heard someone say, "What a way to spend my day off. Why did they pick Saturday for a funeral?"

"Shush," someone said back.

Pastor Wenck began the typical Lutheran funeral service. George Wollenberg's friends received both Law and Gospel, and Wenck hoped they were listening! When he finished and as everyone filed out of the room, Andy noticed someone there he did not expect- Stan Peters! Peters went over to Martha and Andy could not hear, but they looked like something was up. Then, Stan slipped something into her hand; an envelope. He put on his hat and began to walk out. And so did she! "Why would the widow walk out and leave all these people there and not even go to the cemetery?" he muttered to himself. Then it dawned on him. She was going to leave all right- for good! Trying to make his way to the door was impossible for the crowd and she had already gone out. Thinking quickly, he walked through the embalming room and out the back exit. There, getting into a cab was Martha, suitcase and all! Running after her was no use. She had gotten away!

When Andy got back to the station, he told Capt. Peterson the whole story on Martha. Peterson got on the phone right away. "Yes, your Honor. We don't want cop killers on the loose. Thank you, Sir." He hung up and said to Andy, "She won't get far Andy. The whole country will know about Martha now."

Andy went back to his desk and wondered where Martha had gone. When Martha got off the train in Buffalo, she had no one to meet her. She picked up the one suitcase she had and started down the track toward the exit. But a strap had fallen out of her heavy suitcase and was dragging along the sidewalk. It was snowing and instead of taking the time to open her case and stuff it in she just let it drag. It was an unfortunate mistake. When she got to the cab stand she hailed a cab and made her way to the curb. Three or four cabs went by her in a rush and as she tried to get close she tripped on the strap into the path of a cab. When the cabbie was questioned he said he never saw her, just a bright light that he said shone like the sun coming up! She never made it to the hospital or Nova Scotia!

Chapter Twenty-Three- Bye-Bye Betty!

Hal called Tony into the living room, “Say Tony, would you bring me a bottle of that white wine we got the other day?”

“Sure, Boss,” he answered, and bringing it in with three glasses, sat by the fire and took out the cork. Giving each of them an equal amount, Tony handed them to Hal and Ned who was wondering why the wine.

“A toast,” said Hal.

“To what, Boss?”

“A toast to the man who has more than paid for his wages- to Ned.”

“To Ned,” said Tony, and they each took a swig.

Ned was embarrassed and said. “I haven’t done anything.”

“Oh, but you will, and I just put your second month’s salary in the bank.”

“Thanks, Hal.”

“But how about you pick some of the winners for tonight and I’ll let you earn your keep. Huh?”

“Sure, Hal,” and Ned picked up the paper and got started.

When he finished he gave it to Hal and Hal gave it to Tony. “Make it big tonight, I have a hunch.”

“Sure will, Boss.” As Tony started to leave, Hal picked up the paper Ned used to make the picks.

Ned called after Tony before he left the room. “Say Tony, could I speak with you?” Ned got up and the two walked toward the kitchen. “Could I get into a little of the, what do you call it, “action”?”

Tony was taken aback and laughed. “Sure, Ned. What kind of bet you want?”

“I don’t know. Just use about two-hundred on any of the ones I gave Hal.”

"You got it, Ned." And off he went.

It was late and Betty was tired. She got in the tub and just relaxed. Suddenly, the door to the bathroom flew open and the light went out. A single shot was fired and Betty was dead. The silhouette of a man with a hat standing in front of the window was seen by the neighbor just before the light went out. But he never thought anything of it, until he heard the shot. Then he called police. "This is Bob Davis. I live on Jessamine across the alley from Betty Rippentrop. I just heard a shot and the saw the shadow of a man in a hat. I know her husband died, so there shouldn't be anyone like that there."

"OK. OK," said Scully, "We'll send someone over there right away." What Bob didn't see was the Pontiac with the Red Cross sticker drive away out in front.

"MALONE!!!" shouted Capt. Peterson when he saw him come in the office.

Andy threw his coat on his chair and headed in. "Yes, Captain?"

"We just got a call from someone over on Jessamine. Says there's been a shot fired at a woman named Betty Rippentrop's house? Ever heard of her?"

"Oh my! I was going to question her in the morning about her husband. He was the one killed in the Concordia fire."

"BUT HE WASN"T KILLED IN THE FIRE!" screamed the Capt. at Andy. Cross just said he was murdered before the fire. Do I have to do your job for you Malone? Get over there and find out what happened!"

"Yes, Sir," said a puzzled Malone as he jogged out to his coat and toward the door. "Who went out to Rippentrop's, Scully?" Andy asked.

"Roller!" he yelled as Andy flew by and out the door.

Roller walked slowly to the front door revolver in hand. The door was ajar and he pushed it open slowly. It squeaked and he just pushed it open announcing his presence, "This is Officer Roller, come out with your hands up!" But no one came. He turned on the light to the living room- nothing. He turned on the light to the kitchen- nothing. He went over to the bathroom and turned on the light. "Oh, Betty," he said. There, lying in a pool of blood was Betty. He quickly felt for signs of life- nothing. She was dead. Roller used her phone to call for backup. "Scully, send some backup will ya? Betty Rippentrop has been shot and she's dead. Tell Cross."

"Andy's on his way," replied Scully.

When Andy arrived, the two cops did a sweep of the house- nothing. The place was clean, like she almost shot herself. There was no gun, no note, no- nothing. "Whoever did this knew what they were doing," said Roller.

"Sure looks that way," replied Andy.

"What does this all mean, Andy?"

"Yeah, I don't know, and it won't be long and we won't have anybody left to question."

"You got that right!"

The next morning, Andy called Pastor Wenck. Jen answered. "Good morning, Concordia Lutheran."

"This is Officer Malone. Is Pastor Wenck there?"

"No, I'm sorry but something came up with the Rippentrop funeral and he had to go to the funeral parlor."

"Which funeral?" asked Andy.

"What do you mean officer, which funeral?"

"I mean Gerhard or Betty?"

"WHAT?" she exclaimed, and it sounded like she dropped the phone.

"Jen? Are you there?"

"Yes, for a moment I thought you inferred Betty was dead."

"I hate to tell you Jen, but she is. Found shot in her home last night."

"Oh my Lord! So many people dying this way. Carl will just be horrified."

"Would you have him call when he comes in?"

"Sure, Officer. Goodbye."

Andy hung up and called Jim Cross. "Say Jim, I heard that Gerhard was dead before the fire. What was the cause of death?"

"A bullet to the head, Andy. But that's not all I found. He had 10-G's on him."

"Wow. Ten-thousand bucks, huh?"

"Yeah. Where does a mason get that kind of dough?"

"We'll find out I guess- someday." They both hung up. What Cross said wasn't true though. Gerhard had 15-G's on him and he had skimmed 5-G's for himself!

None of it made any sense to him. Andy was out of ideas. Why all the deaths? Why burn the church? Why? Why? Why? He needed a new game plan- a new approach. A new…then the phone rang. "Andy, this is Sam Goodhall, FBI."

"Why hello, G-Man, how are ya?"

"Fine. Fine. I got another lead on that Hal Howard for you. It seems that he left Florida for the North somewhere. As he is from Chicago we'll start there, but I think if you have anywhere there to stake out you should."

"Thanks, Sam! You're the greatest!"

"Don't mention it."

They both hung up and Andy yelled out to Scully, "Hey Scully! Come here!"

"What do you want? Can't you see I'm busy?"

"Have we got anyone for a long stakeout?"

"Whadda ya mean- long?"

"Oh, a few days at the most."

"Just- Salomenson."

"Good. Send him over to stakeout the Overlook Apartment Penthouse. We may have a lead on Ned again!"

Tony came into the room and showed Hal a piece of paper. Hal just grinned and said, "See? I told you so!"

Tony walked over to Ned and said, "Good job, Ned."

"What do you mean, Tony?"

"You made the boss half a million last night."

"What? Really? I didn't know you could bet that much!"

"We didn't. You just hit ALL the numbers," said Hal.

"Won't the people you bet with get suspicious, Hal?"

"Yes, they might. But that's why we lost last time. And that's what we are gonna continue to do until I can play one that is so huge, I'll own them all!"

'So that's the plan,' Ned thought, 'to own the whole syndicate.'

"Next time, Ned, there's a bonus in it for you. Don't let it be said I don't take care of my old army buddies!" Hal slapped Ned on the back and walked toward the bathroom.

Meanwhile, Pastor Wenck was distraught. When he found out about Betty's death he could not be consoled. Another funeral like that was just too much. Jen brought in the mail. He looked at it and noticed an envelope. It was an envelope just like the other one- the one that had money in it. Could it be? He got out his letter opener this time not wanting to tear anything that may be in it. Sure enough, this one had money, too! It contained $4,650.00 in cash. Exactly the same amount as last month and on the exact day. It was like someone was sending in an offering every month. "Thank you

Lord for this blessing, but tell us what it means?" He jumped when his phone rang. 'That was quick,' he thought to himself.

Sven was on the other end of the line. "Hallo, Pastor. I know it's not a good time wit all da funerals and such, but we have jus one more bowling tournament dis week, don't ja know. Vill you be dare?"

"I know how much this last one means to you all, Sven. Even though I have a lot on my plate, you know you can always count on me."

"Tanks, Pastor. See you on Friday!"

Chapter Twenty-Four- Olaf Makes another Bet

"Andy, this is Pastor Wenck. Jen told me about Betty and I've already got her next of kin contacted. But..." The preacher had thought he'd better call him and report this new development with the money in the mail. One time was unusual enough, but two?

"Oh hello Pastor, thanks for returning my call. But? What's up?"

"I thought I better tell you about another unusual occurrence here at Concordia."

"What can be more unusual than what's been happening there lately?" Andy mused.

Wenck told him all about the two envelopes full of money. "Well, no laws have been broken, unless we were to find out the money was stolen. But until such time that we do, the money is rightly the churches'."

"That's what I thought, but I wanted you to know about it."

"Thanks for the information, Pastor."

"Oh, Andy, just to let you know. Betty will be interred on Wednesday."

"OK. I'll be there. Goodbye."

Jim Cross walked in and handed Andy a couple of reports. "It's the ballistics reports on Gerhard and Betty."

"And what do they say?"

"Same caliber and same gun- a 357 magnum."

"No fooling around there. OK, so we know the gun. Thanks, Jim."

"You bet, Andy." As Cross walked back to the basement he smiled and said to himself, "Keep them coming, Andy. I'll get rich if you do!"

Olaf had gone back to work after Olga's funeral to forget. He worked extra hours at the brewery and the boss had begun to notice him. The bad thing was that Olaf's boss, Hank, was not the kind of man that he should hang around with. In fact, he was a friend of Vic and at times Vic used him as muscle to collect some of the "script" money he was owed. "Say Olaf, what are you going to do with all the extra money you've been making lately?"

"Oh, I jus been saving it for da rainy day, don't ya know."

"What? Saving it you say? I know a better way to make money with it than that! That lousy bank gives you what, 3% a month? Ha, I can get you 50% or even 100% on your investment. All you have to do is….and that's all there is to it."

Olaf listened to Hank's entire spiel and he was very interested, especially since his bet with Evan. "Oh ja, I place da bet before. Wit Evan O'Reilly. I win towsands."

"Thousands you say? Where is this money now?"

"In da bank!"

"Oh yeah, the bank," the boss replied. "Well, bring it and we'll turn it into some serious money."

"I tink about it," said Olaf and he went back to his post on the line.

Ned was getting bored. Besides an occasional bet with part of the money Hal was giving him, he'd just been sitting in the window every day looking out at the park and watching the world go by. His bright spot of the day was when he could read the paper when Tony brought it in each morning. Today he picked it up and saw the news, "Woman murdered in own tub!" He found the headline to be sensational until he read the name, Betty Rippentrop! "HAL!" he yelled, "HAL! Betty's been murdered!"

Tony came running back into the kitchen. Hal came equally as fast and both men arrived at the same time to look over Ned's shoulder. "What did you say? Where? Betty?"

"Yes- Betty! They found her shot in her tub!"

Hal grabbed the paper from Ned and said, "Let me see that! You're right. And it says they have no information or leads as to who could have done it. It sounds fishy to me. Like one of the boys did it."

"Yeah, Boss," chimed in Tony.

"Tony, go over there and see what you can find. Be careful."

"OK, Boss."

In front of the window Salomensen saw the whole thing. When Tony left to go to Betty's, he followed him.

Andy was on his way to the YMCA to see the director when he saw them, Tony on the street walking toward Jessamine and Salomensen behind him about a half-block. Andy said to himself, "What is he doing?" Looking in his rear view mirror, he saw Tony cross the street, grab a cab, and leave the cop stranded with no one to follow. Andy muttered, "Serves him right, he wasn't supposed to follow anyone. He blew his cover." Andy whipped around in the black and white and tried to follow the cab. They went a couple of blocks with the cab in sight, but to no avail, Andy lost him, too. Tony looked behind him. He smiled and sat back.

When they got two blocks away from Betty's house, he had the cab let him out. Giving the cabbie a twenty he said, "Keep da change." The snow crunched under his feet as he walked. He noticed that by this time of day there were few cars parked on the street in front of these houses. Working families lived there. When he got to her house, he saw that the cops had sealed the front door. Looking around to make sure he wasn't being observed, he walked through a neighbor's yard and to the alley. The back door was not posted or sealed, so he took out his pick key set and opened the door. For sure, Tony knew how to break into a house! He looked around to find the same thing the cops found- nothing. Except- there on the bathroom floor behind the door was a thread. "They must have missed it," he said to himself. It looked like mohair. He put it in his shirt pocket. Tony looked up and out the bathroom window. The neighbor, Bob Davis, had seen him go in and was coming towards the back door!

Tony got out his gun and went toward the front of the house to hide. Bob tried to open the back door, but Tony had closed and locked it on his way in. Bob wasn't going to break in so he went back to his house to call the cops.

Quickly, Tony ran out the back door. Seeing this occur from his kitchen window, Bob handed the phone to his wife Doris to call the cops and he ran out to chase Tony. He didn't know what he was in for. Being without transportation, Tony ran down the alley. Bob came around the corner of his garage and when he did he yelled at the thug. "Hey you! What were you doing in there?" Tony didn't respond except to pull out his gun and fire two rounds at the guy. Bang! Bang! Bob ducked. The two rounds whizzed past his head. Lucky for him, Tony missed.

By the time the cops got there, all was quiet. Tony had walked the alleys to Frogtown and was cold by the time he was able to get a cab. The cops drove around looking for this intruder to no avail. They were just too late. When Andy left the meeting at the YMCA, he heard the news about the break in. He arrived to find a shivering Bob Davis at Betty's house with Roller. "He went into the house just like he lived here. No forced entry or nothing. The house is clean too, just like we left it, Andy," said Roller.

"Did you get a good look at him, Bob?" asked Andy.

"Pretty good. But when he shot at me, I got out of the way." Andy looked at Roller.

"Yeah Andy, two rounds," said Roller.

"Well, if there's nothing here, let's seal the back door and go home. Thanks for the call, Bob, and don't go near the place if you see anything again! Just call us."

"You can bet on that!" said the frightened witness.

Instead of going back to the penthouse, Tony took the cab to the pharmacy to hang out with Vic. He called Hal to let him know where he was. Then, he asked about what bet he wanted him to place for the night. "Ned says Duke over Rutgers 55-29."

"OK, Boss. Be back soon." When he walked in the back, Hank was there. "Hi, Tony! How ya doin?", and Hank slapped him on the back.

"Great, Hank. Where's Vic?"

"He's in front with the pharmacist. He'll be right back."

"So, what's new, Hank?"

"I thought I'd come in and tell Vic about this new patsy I found at work. The Swede has "towsands" and I'm gonna make him bet!"

"What's the guys' name?"

"His name is Olaf Tschida. Why?"

"That guy! I know him! He bet O'Reilly on a bowling score and won. O'Reilly felt sorry for him because he was stealing his girl and gave him a pot of money before he left the country. What a joke!"

"So that's how he got it. Ha! Well, we can remedy that! Leave it to the pharmacy to heal all your woes!" They just laughed.

Vic came into the back room. "Hi, Tony. What's new?"

"I just cased the Rippentrop house. Betty worked for Hal, ya know. You guys got any idea who did it?"

Vic and Hank looked at each other. Vic said slowly, "No Tony, we don't."

Tony, sensing a lie just kept going. "Well if you hear anything, da Boss would like to know. That's all."

A knock came to the back door. Hank looked out the peep hole. It was Olaf and he let him in. "Come out of the cold, Olaf, and take off your coat."

Olaf walked in and put his coat on a chair. Uncomfortable, he looked around and just waited until someone said something to him.

"Well, Olaf, what are you going to try your luck at?" asked Hank.

"Vell I like da basketball games, so I tink I go for dat."

"Here's a list of the games. Take your time! Ha, ha," he laughed.

After Hank left him, Tony went over to Olaf. As Tony was kind of upset that Vic and Hank were holding something back about Betty, he thought he'd teach them a lesson.

"Say Olaf, my name is Tony. I heard from a reliable source that Duke was going to beat Rutgers tonight. In fact, he said the score would be 55-29. Trust me. You can't lose with this."

"Ya don't say? OK, I put da bet on dat." Olaf walked over and placed the bet.

Vic said, "Good luck, Olaf. If you win with this kind of bet you'll be a rich man."

"Tank you. I hope to vin, too, don't ya know."

Tony came up to Olaf and asked, "Say Olaf, how much did you bet on that game?"

"Oh, two towsand dollars."

Tony laughed. "Well, if you are right, you *will* be a rich man."

Making sure he was in the earshot of Vic he said to Olaf, "If you need help getting these guys to pay up, just let me know." Tony opened the door for Olaf and they walked out into the cold night air.

"Tanks, Tony", said Olaf as they parted.

"Don't mention it, Olaf."

Tony walked the ten blocks to the Overlook Apts. When he got to the penthouse, Hal was there waiting for him. "Where have you been?"

"It's a long story, Boss."

"Well go ahead and tell me. I got plenty of time."

So, Tony told him the whole story. All about the thread, the nosey neighbor, the shots, and Olaf. What intrigued him the most was the reaction Tony had gotten from Vic and Hank. "Yeah, Boss and ya know what I did?"

"No, I don't Tony, tell me."

"I told Olaf how to place his bet with some numbers from Ned."

Hal laughed and laughed about that one! "Serves them right! But ya know, Tony, we gotta watch them and find out about this Betty thing."

"Damn right, Boss!"

Chapter Twenty-Five- At Funeral Three Malone gets close

Pastor Wenck got out of his Plymouth and walked over to the door of the mortuary. He was visibly shaken. So many funerals under these circumstances made it impossible for him to sleep. And the fire and its aftermath gave him more reasons to pray. When he opened the door, Franz the mortician, welcomed him in. "Good morning, Herr Pastor! You look tired this Wednesday morning."

"I am. I have not been able to sleep well lately, Franz."

"Do not be discouraged, Pastor. The Lord has His ways and we will someday look back and see what and how He has blessed us."

"Thank you, Franz. What you say is so true. Let us never forget that." Carl walked over to the casket and looked at Betty. She looked just like she did the other day when she came in to arrange Gerhard's funeral. Carl wondered so many things about this situation and that's one reason why he wasn't able to sleep. The other was the money. But he had now decided, under the guidance of Franz, to leave it all to the Lord. It would all work out!

As he walked to the front to place his message on the lectern, a couple of people began to come in to view the body. He looked up and nodded, and then noticed someone he had never met before. The old woman sat down in the back, frilly handkerchief in her hand to wipe away her tears. She appeared to be at least ninety years old and very frail. When he finished his preparations, Wenck went back to greet the woman. "Hello, my name is Pastor Carl Wenck. I don't believe I've met you before."

"No, Pastor, you have not. I am Betty's mother, Abigail Mortenson."

"Why, I didn't know she had a mother. I just assumed that because she never mentioned you, or that you were no longer with us."

"We were not close. We have not spoken in fifty years."

"May I sit and talk with you?"

"Yes, please. Even though we were not close, I still loved my daughter." She went on to tell the clergyman all about their falling out, their lack of communication, and the remorse she felt for the whole affair. "What she didn't know is that I had gotten her job for her."

"I didn't know she worked!" replied the surprised clergyman.

"Yes, for a very important man from my hometown, a Mr. Hal Howard. He has a penthouse in downtown St. Paul."

"I see. I guess I just assumed she was retired as well. Sometimes we don't get to know our parishioners as well as we ought."

Behind the two and out of their sight sat Andy, listening to this interesting conversation. He about jumped out of his skin when he heard it! But playing it cool, he just sat there as more and more people filed in for the service. Finally, the preacher excused himself and proceeded back to the front to begin. Andy sat listening to the service and watching those that came in. Arriving late a man in a mohair coat sat across from him. It was him again, Stan Peters! Then coming in from the front side sat a big man he knew he had seen before and next to him, a dignified man in an Italian suit. Who was it?

After Pastor prayed and excused the crowd, Andy watched to see who would greet one another. Sure enough, Stan Peters went forward to greet the man in the front and then the man in the front went back to greet- Abigail! The big guy stood beside him with his arms crossed. Andy could tell he was his body guard. Slowly and with great care, the big guy helped Abigail up and toward the door.

Andy went out to the parking lot while the three waited and talked. Then Andy saw it, the Caddie from Illinois! Then it hit him, it was Hal Howard! As Tony was out at the car and he was in his civvies, he thought he may as well try to take him in for questioning. He made his way toward the door and the small group. As he did Pastor Wenck came up to him and said, "Officer Malone, could I speak with you?" As soon as Hal heard this, leaving Stan Peters and Abigail to run interference for him, he made his way out the door and to the Caddie. As Andy excused himself from Pastor Wenck and got out to the parking lot it was too late, AGAIN!!! Now he knew Ned was probably in town!

"I knew we shouldn't have gone, Boss," said Tony as they drove away.

"Yeah, yeah, you're always right. I guess I should have figured the cops would be there. Let's go get Ned and head out of town. They're on the way by now and we'll have to make it snappy."

Hal was right. Andy had already called the station and Roller and Salomensen were on their way. When the Caddie pulled up to the door, the Black and White was right on their tail. Tony just kept on going. Roller wondered if they saw it right. "Is that them?"

"It's an Illinois' Caddie ain't it? Follow them!" So Roller kept on going, too! Tony was still a better driver than Roller and by the time they got to the state line, Tony didn't even see his headlights anymore.

"Good job, Tony. Let's go to Hudson tonight."

"OK, Boss. And Boss?"

"Yeah, Tony?"

"Did you see Peters' coat?"

"What about it?"

"It was mohair."

"Good eye, Tony. So he was the one that killed Betty. Wonder why?"

"And what about Ned?"

"Ah, he'll be alright. Besides, he's probably asleep by now."

But he wasn't asleep. In fact, Ned had made his way down to the lobby. He had packed the clothes he had and was making a break for it! When he started to the front door, Blythe caught up to him. "Excuse me, Sir, but I must inform you that Mr. Howard has asked me to detain you if you were to try to leave without an escort."

"Is that so?" And with that, Ned let him have it with his cane! Thud went the Englishman to the floor. Glancing down at him Ned said, "I'm so sorry Blythe, but I just can't stay!" Picking up his suitcase, he walked out the door to freedom. He'd only made it a block and he began to be winded. He sat his suitcase down under a streetlight by the entrance to the park that he had seen below his window.

A car slowly pulled up next to him and the window came down in the back. It was *her!* It was the "most beautiful" woman he had seen get out of the car the other day! She asked, "Need a lift?" All he could do is nod his head. When Ned was safely in the car and the bearded chauffeur had placed his suitcase in the trunk, he drove slowly away. She then asked, "Where are you going?"

"I really don't know," he said, "anywhere away from here. What's your name?" he asked.

"I'm Ida. What's your name?"

"I'm Ned. Nice to meet you."

He watched streetlight after streetlight fade past as the car went over the bridge. He asked, "Are we in Wisconsin?"

"Yes, we're in Hudson. There's a nice cottage there I go to from time to time. We're going there."

"Oh, OK," he said smiling. When the car pulled up the chauffer let them out and they went up to the door. The Innkeeper let them in and gave them a key. No words were spoken and they made their way back out the covered walkway to cabin five. The river steamed in the cold night air and a mist hung over the roof. This was not ordinary cabin. It looked huge from the outside. More like a house to Ned. When they got to the door and started to open it, it swung open and there stood- Tony! Ned just stood there jaw on the floor and the woman walked past them and over to Hal who stood behind Tony. She put her arms around him and gave him a hug. "Nice of you to join us, Ned," said Hal.

Back in St. Paul, Andy walked into the lobby of the Overlook after parking the black and white. He found Blythe just waking from his encounter with Ned. Picking him up from the floor Andy asked, "Do you want to tell me what's going on here or do you want to do it at the station?"

"He won't like it."

"Who won't like it?"

"Mr. Howard. He does not take stoolies lightly."

"You have no choice, either tell, or go to jail."

"Very well." He stood up, straightened his clothes and smoothed back his hair. When he did, he felt the wound and bump on his head. "Ouch!"

"Who did that to you?"

"I'm not at liberty to say."

"Well, you had better think about what I just said. Either you talk or you have many more lumps than that!"

"You wouldn't dare!"

"I didn't say me. If you think Tony is big, you should see Robinson at the station!"

Blythe sat down. "Mr. Oelker hit me with his cane."

"Where is he?"

"I don't know. He left after he hit me, I presume with the suitcase he was carrying."

"And Hal Howard?"

"I have not seen Mr. Howard, nor his man Tony since they left to attend a funeral this afternoon."

"Let's go to the penthouse. I want to see if they may come back."

"If we do, officer, I do not wish to go down on record as having let you in."

"No problem, mate!"

"Oh dear," sighed Blythe.

"I'm sorry, Hal. It's just been so long since I've been out. I couldn't resist it under the circumstances."

"I totally understand, Ned. In fact, I think we ought to change a few things. If I can trust you to be just like any other employee, you can trust me to be just like any other boss. The only difference is that we stick together like family. Got it?"

"Got it. And I can go out?"

"Sure, as long as one of us goes with you to help you."

"Oh. Well, OK."

Hal came over to Ned and put his arm around his shoulder and pointed him toward the kitchen. "The first thing I want you to do is make me a coffee cake for breakfast."

"Really?"

"Yes, do what you do best, Ned."

"Thanks, Hal!"

Ned was shown to his room and unpacked his bag. Tony knocked on the door. "Can I come in, Ned?" he asked.

"Sure, Tony."

"Ya know, Ned, he really doesn't want to make you feel like a prisoner. He wants this to work out for the best. Do you understand?"

Ned felt the compassion in Tony's words. "I know, Tony. We've been friends for a long time. I just have a hard time with not going out. I get cabin fever easy. That's all."

"It's just the cops. Ya know?"

"Well, we'll be more careful now won't we?"

"You bet," said Tony happily. "Do we need anything in the kitchen?"

"I'll find out."

Ned went straight to the kitchen and looked around. "This is great for a "cottage" kitchen. It has all I need to get to work." And to work he went. Within a couple of hours he had the coffee cake ready to bake in the morning and he had prepared a dinner for the whole group. Ned called out, "Soups on!" Hal and Ida came out to the kitchen and sat at the table. Tony came in and helped Ned get it all on the table.

"What smells so good, Ned?" asked Ida.

"It's clam chowder and homemade biscuits. And for desert is an apple cobbler I just threw together."

"I told you we were glad to have you join us, Ned," mused Hal. They all laughed and dug in. Hal was glad to see Ned more at ease. He hoped it would be like that when he told him what he had planned for next week.

Vic looked at the result of the games and saw the impossible. Olaf had won the bet. He won the bet? It couldn't be! The Boss was going to be mad. It meant that he'd have to come up with 48 grand! "Why me? Why is it always me? You'd think that once that old guy was gone this wouldn't happen anymore," he said to himself.

Hank had heard about it and had come over to the pharmacy. "What you gonna do Vic?"

"Pay it. What else can I do? If I don't, I'll lose all my customers. Olaf is going to be a rich man."

"We can change that, too."

Vic looked at him and smiled. Then he laughed and said, "You mean like Gerhard and his fifteen grand?" Hank smiled and they both laughed.

"What are you two laughing about," asked the Boss as he came into the room.

"Oh nothing, Mr. Peters," the two replied.

Chapter Twenty-Six- "Stiffed" and "Freed"

Ned sat in a chair sipping coffee by the fireplace, while Tony washed the dishes and Hal played pool in the parlor. Ida had excused herself to lounge in the master bath tub. As the flames danced and darted, logs crackling from time to time, Ned thought about the life he had led since Suzie's death. He had been lonely. All he did was go to work at Tschida's, go to watch the bowlers and basketball games, an occasional hockey game, and church. Not that it was all that bad of a life, but there was something missing. He knew it was -Suzie. But she was gone. So, if this new life is what was supposed to be, Malachi would tell him. At least he thought so. Tony came and sat down in the chair across from him. "Thanks for doing the dishes, Tony."

"Thanks for making such a good meal, Ned. It was the least I could do."

Ned opened up and started to confide in Tony. "Ya know Tony, I was just thinking. When I came to be in this situation, I was scared. I didn't know what to make of it under the circumstances. But now, I don't feel that way. I feel more like a part of a family, even if we do things that aren't considered- "lawful"."

"It ain't that bad. But we do have to move around a lot. The cops don't like us much."

"Well, I like you."

"Thanks, Ned."

Olaf knocked on the back door of the pharmacy. "Oh, it's you," said Vic as he let him in.

Olaf seemed excited as he walked in and said, "I come to pick up my vinnings, Vic. How much I vin?"

"You vin," he corrected himself, "you *won*- forty-eight grand, Olaf. I'll go get it. It's in the safe."

“Forty-eight towsand dollars!” Olaf screamed, “YAHOO! I gonna buy a house and go into business for myself and try to find a good woman dis time.”

“Ya, sure,” replied Vic as he stacked the money so Olaf could count it. When he got done, Olaf put it all in a sack and started out the door. “Hey, Olaf.”

“Ya, Vic?”

“Aren’t you gonna bet any of that?”

“Oh ya sure, but I gonna wait until I tink about it.”

“Oh yeah, you tink about it.” Vic laughed.

Olaf walked out and down toward Swede Hollow. He didn’t see Hank behind him in the dark. When he rounded a corner there was a man straight in front of him. Then a man behind him. He got scared and started to try to get by them. The man in front tried to grab his sack of money. The man behind, hit him with a lead pipe. Thunk! Thunk, thunk, thunk, rang out the swats to his head. Olaf lay in the snow bleeding profusely from his wounds. The thugs took the cash and ran to a car parked on the next street and tore away from the scene of the crime.

By the time Olaf was found in the morning, he had frozen to death. A garbage man found him covered with a couple inches of snow. “At first I thought he was just asleep, but when I saw the frozen blood underneath, I knew he was probably dead,” said the worker.

“Thanks,” said Inspector Dumont, “you can go.”

Andy, having been alerted to a crime, came walking up to the scene just as they were putting Olaf on a stretcher. “What have we got Inspector?”

“Murdered brewery worker. Not sure of the motive, but it may have been robbery. We found a pack of twenties in the snow under him.”

“Got an ID?”

“Yeah, his name is Olaf Tschida.”

"OH NO!" Andy exclaimed.

"Know him?"

"Yeah. Good kid. I'll take care of notifying the next of kin."

"Thanks, Andy." The two parted, each going to do their jobs.

Pastor answered the door and let Andy in. "Pastor, I have more bad news for you and this is going to be difficult. Olaf is dead."

"Oh dear Lord." Carl sunk to the bench seat in the foyer of his home. "I'd like it if you came along with me to tell Sven."

Standing up and wiping back a tear he said, "Let's go. But for once, I am at a loss for words."

When they got to the bakery, Sven was in the back with his new helper, Capt. Peterson's wife, Ava. The cashier was new too, but Andy didn't know her. "Hello. I'm Officer Andy Malone. I'd like to see Sven when he has a minute."

"Oh Ya, for sure. I'm Heidi Jungeman. I go tell him." She walked to the back and came out with Sven.

"Oh hallo, Pastor Carl und Andy! What can I do for you?"

Andy said very seriously, "Sven could we see you in your office? We'd like to talk."

Sven's demeanor changed and he knew something was wrong. He took off his apron and said, "Ya sure, come mit me." They walked over to a side door of the back room and up a set of stairs to a backroom office behind the apartment Sven had lived in for forty years. Sven sat down. "Sit down my friends. Is dare something wrong?"

Andy stayed standing and Pastor Wenck went over to stand by Sven. "Sven, its Olaf. They found him dead in Swede Hollow this morning. He was beaten and robbed."

Sven began to sob. “Oh no. Oh no.” His head hit his pastor’s arm and Carl held him as they both cried. “He is my only son, my only son.”

“Sven, do you have any idea why he would be there last night?”

“No. He usually go home and read. He read a lot, especially da Gud Book.”

“Have any idea how he got this money?” Andy showed him the stack of twenties neatly bundled.

“No. How much is dat?”

“It’s five hundred dollars.”

“No. But he had some money he and Olga were going to use and maybe he take it from da bank.”

“Maybe. I’m sorry, Sven. Could you come downtown today to identify his body?”

“Ya. I come.”

“And Pastor Carl, would you begin arrangements for Sven?”

“I will. I don’t know what I’m going to tell the congregation. This will hit them hard, especially with all of the others in the past month. This is worse than the 1920’s!”

Like always, Tony sat the paper by Ned and walked over for a cup of coffee. The coffee cake was almost done baking and the aroma was wafting throughout the cottage. It brought the others in single file to the kitchen. Ned opened the paper and looked at the headline. “Local Brewery worker beaten to death.” Ned knew lots of men that worked at the brewery. He went over to take the baked delight out of the oven. Tony glanced at the front page and read the first few lines. He turned white and read it out loud. “The worker, Olaf Tschida, was found covered with new fallen snow in a pool of blood.” Ned and Tony in unison muttered, “Oh My!”

Hal said, “You guys know him?”

“Yeah, Boss, remember? I saw him over at Vic’s and he made a bet?”

"Oh, yeah. Say, I bet those bums did this!"

"Yeah. I bet they paid him off and stole it back. Then, they killed him."

"I hope Peters stayed out of it, I told him to keep low."

Ned was so upset when he heard all this, he went back to his room to lay down. He looked in the drawer for a Bible. He found it and opened to the book of Malachi. After reading for a bit, he fell asleep. He heard a voice. "Do not be weary. For the Lord says, "All the arrogant and the evildoer will be stubble."" When Ned woke up it was late in the afternoon. Ned looked at the verse open on the page. It was Malachi, Chapter four, verse one...

He heard a car door slam and looked out the frost framed window. Tony was out warming up the car. Ida was standing next to him smoking a cigarette. Hal came out and the three of them got in and drove away. 'Huh. Hal must really trust me,' he thought. Ned went out in the hallway by the phone. There was a note sitting on the table. "Dear Ned, We went into town to see about this whole thing. Try to think of something we all can do for the family. Signed, Hal". He thought, 'Maybe he does care. Maybe God has softened his heart.' Ned picked up the phone and started to dial. But, he stopped and hung up and went out to the kitchen for a snack. He didn't need to call. He *was, in effect, free*. God and his angel were indeed looking out for him.

Tony drove past the brewery to see if Hanks' car was in the parking lot. It was and Tony knew the whistle blew at four-thirty. So, he drove over to the pharmacy to see Vic. Hal knocked on the door. Vic hurried to let him in. Surprised, he stuttered when he said, "HeHehelloo, Boss."

"Hello, Vic. I heard there was a little trouble around here last night."

"Trouble?"

"Don't play dumb with me! You know what trouble! Tony!"

At that, Tony went over and picked up Vic by the collar and dragged him into the office out of sight of the rest of the boys. Hal slammed the door.

"Did you have anything to do with that robbery and murder?" Hal asked.

Vic said, "Boss, I didn't want to do it! It was Hank's idea!"

Hal snapped his fingers and Tony broke first his right arm, then his left. Vic bent over in complete and total agony. Tony said, "The boss expects all the money back by five. Call us at the cottage."

They left Vic in his office, went back to the car, and headed toward Hudson.

One of Vic's boys came into the office. Vic said, "Call Peters and then get the car. I gotta go to the hospital. And get Hank over here right away!"

Hank got the phone call in his office. "WHAT! The Boss came in and did what? OK. I'll get it. But I ain't sticking around. Yeah, Bye." Hank and Bruno, his henchman, got in his Cadillac and drove down Rice Street, and then headed north to Canada. He stopped in White Bear Lake to fill up. After placing the nozzle in the car, the attendant went in to answer the phone. Bruno got out and started to talk to Hank. "You suppose Hal will try to catch us?"

"Try? Huh. You dope! If we don't get out of the country we're dead men! Even if we do, we still might be!" Bruno got out his cigarettes. Unwittingly he took out his Zippo and flicked it open. When Hank figured out what he was doing it was too late. Bruno rolled the flint wheel and BOOM! The fumes from the gas ignited in a huge fireball!

Ned heard the Caddie drive up and the doors slam shut. Ida wasn't with Hal and Tony. "Whew it's cold out there. Ida says goodbye. I had to take her to the train," said Hal as he hurriedly shut the door and took off his coat and gloves. He looked across the room to see Ned staring at the fire.

Ned looked up and said, "I think I know what we can do. Sven has always wanted the bakery to be paid off so he didn't have to worry."

"Done!" said Hal.

"He isn't getting any younger and Olaf was his only son."

Tony and Hal looked at each other as if to say, "Look what this business does to people."

Ned said, "I think I'll get ready to go to Olaf's funeral. You two going?"

Tony and Hal looked at each other again. "Do you think that is wise, Ned?"

"Maybe you're right. How about if I just go to the cemetery?"

Tony looked at Hal and said, "I'll drive you, Ned."

The two men waited around the corner from Michoetti's until the funeral procession went by toward the cemetery. Ned felt bad he was not there to comfort Sven. When they got to the cemetery, there were few mourners left. It was cold. Ned waited until the group was up to the grave and he walked up close enough to hear Pastor Wenck speak. He heard the group say, "Amen." Then the crank on the lift began to lower Olaf into his final resting place. He stepped back enough for them to not notice him behind a tree. When they were all gone he went up to the casket and placed a flower on Olaf's grave. Ned cried for his friend. Tony came to help him back to the car.

Sven sat down to eat his supper. He looked out over Rice Street and watched the traffic. It was one of his favorite things to do. He loved American cars, The Fords, Chevies, and Cadillacs. His favorite was Packard. But, he didn't even own a car. Living on Rice Street made it easy to walk everywhere he needed to go. There was even a supermarket two blocks down. But who needed those?

The lutefisk was getting old. He was glad he was eating the last of it. He, Olaf, and the family had it for Christmas. His sister had come down with her family to celebrate too. Sven missed her, but knew he'd see her in a couple of days after the funeral. He cried again.

As he looked out, a big black Cadillac slowed down and someone in it threw something at the building. Sven thought, 'Oh no they vill break da window!' He got up and ran down the private entrance to the street. But no! There on the doorstep was a newspaper all wrapped up. It looked way too big. He opened it to find a roll of money. It contained forty-eight "towsand" dollars and a note. It said, "This is Olaf's." The next day, Sven got a letter from the bank, and it was a paid-in-full note on the building. He fainted right there in the bakery, his head resting on a ball of dough!

Andy had been so busy he didn't have a chance to follow up on all the leads he had on Ned's case. All the events of late, the murders, the suspicious deaths, seemed to point to the same group of people- Hal Howard and the mob. He had planned on bringing in Stan Peters, so he sent Roller and Salomensen out to pick him up for questioning. Malone's phone rang.

It was Sven. "Hallo dis is Sven Tschida. I tink I have something to report?"

"What is it, Sven?"

"I been having strange happening's here at da Bakery and I vant to show you. Can you come?"

"Sure Sven, but it will be an hour or two."

"Ya sure dat's OK. I be here all day."

Andy hung up and Roller walked in with Peters. "Where's Salomensen?"asked Andy.

"Putting away the car. This guy didn't want to come, Andy."

"Is that so? I thought you were an upstanding citizen, Mr. Peters? What's happened? Getting to close?"

"No comment," he replied, "I'd like my attorney present."

"You do huh? We'll see about that. Take him to the interrogation room, Roller." Roller's eyes lit up and he smiled. He liked that part of his job.

When Roller was done with Peters, they had all the information they needed. It seemed Peters had been skimming off the top from Hal Howard and Howard was getting close to finding out after Wollenberg and the boys killed Gerhard. Then it just got messier and messier. Betty had to be silenced of course. And then there was Olaf and the whole operation at the pharmacy. Peters confessed he was almost glad they had brought him in, but now he was worried he wasn't safe on the inside. They put him in solitary confinement. He had not told them about Sven and the money he had to cough up after Olaf was killed by Hank and Bruno. Peters figured Sven deserved the money. Sven didn't see it that way.

Coroner Cross was a pretty tough guy. He didn't think twice about taking a bribe, or robbing the cadavers when they came in. He didn't think anything of working on a bunch of stiffs. He'd gotten to the point where he'd even eat his lunch while working. A long as no one was around anyway. So, he never got spooked. They were all dead- right? And we all know that the dead don't do nothing. But, when he came in after lunch he thought he heard something. He looked around and saw nothing. Then he heard it again. It sounded like a rattle. The drawer on number three moved. Then drawer two. Then one, four, five and all the rest! He started to get scared. All of a sudden all the drawers flew open and the stiffs sat up! It was all too much for him to take. Cross had a heart attack and fell dead right on the exam table in front of him. When they found him, his bank book was lying next to him with a balance of 400K. They wondered how a coroner could have saved that kind of money. But they knew…

When Andy got to the bakery, Sven took him to the back room and up the stairs to the office. He had a safe there that usually was just left hanging open, but today it was closed and locked. Sven motioned for Andy to take a chair and got down on his knees to open the safe. Spinning the dial, he tried to open it and missed the first time. He said chuckling, "I don't open it very often. I forget da numbers!" When he got it, he pulled out the stack of cash he found with the note. Andy's eyes got big and as he read the note. Sven explained how he got it and asked, "Vat do ve do mit it?"

"I'll take it back to the station for safekeeping and see where it leads. If it is not found to be anyone else's or is claimed, then it will be yours to do with as you please."

"OK. I tink about dat. But what about da paper von da bank?"

"Nothing I can do about that. I think you own a bakery!"

Tony went down to the pharmacy, but took all the back routes just in case. He parked the car under a pine tree in an empty lot nearby. He could hardly tell it was there himself! As he walked toward the building, he noticed something wasn't right. The door was open a crack and light poured out. The front neon light which usually lit the inside of the pharmacy was not on tonight. And there were no cars in the alley when there were usually at least four or five from patrons of Vic's. He smelled a rat and he was right. Just minutes before, the cops had raided the place and taken everyone in. They left two men behind to round up anyone that would happen to come in the rest of the night. Tony went to the front door. It was locked as always at night. He put his mighty hand thru the glass and opened it. The cops didn't hear it because they were listening to the Gopher game on WCCO. Besides, they didn't expect anyone to come in from the front. Tony crept slowly to the back room. Peering in through the peep hole he knew was there in the office, he watched as the cops took a poor, unsuspecting patron into custody. He backed out and put his gun away. When he got to the car it was covered with snow and as he pulled out from under it, the tree exploded in a huge white cloud of powdery winter! He knew it was time to leave St. Paul.

Chapter Twenty-Seven- Ned leaves a clue!

Ned and Hal sat at the kitchen table playing cards. They were generally having a good time- just like the old days! Tony came in and announced, "Time to leave town boss! They just closed down Vic and took everyone that came in downtown!"

Looking at his cards and throwing down a duce Hal said, "Gin."

Ned replied, "That's the third time straight!"

"Are you guys listening?"

Used to the constant moving Hal said, "Yeah, yeah!"

Ned said, "Hal, do you think I could go by the house and pick up some stuff before we go?"

"Sure Ned, why not?"

It took a while for Hal to get the place ready to be closed up now that Betty wasn't around to take care of it for him. It would take a while to find anyone that good. In fact, he might just let the lease run out now that they closed up Vic. But how did they move in so fast on the operation? Someone must have spilled the beans. Ned was packed up and ready to go. He didn't have much to pack after all. He hoped he could get a few more things at the house. He wondered what was going on there. Did they shut off the power and let the place freeze up? Who knew! When Tony finished, they locked the door and headed out the back way. No one saw them leave.

Andy was finishing up questioning the last man brought in from the sting at Vic's. What a day! Now he'd have so many reports to type! And Sergeant Molly Ferguson was not one to let them go either. She'd hound him till they were done, too. She'd have to wait a while with his arm in a sling! He was glad they had finally found what was going on at Vic's and that the place was closed. Too many guys from the Brewery were losing all their paychecks. And he knew Hal and Ned had to be found. He was tired though and knew it was time to go home. He closed his desk and picked up his hat and coat. Going toward the front door he said to Scully, "Do you ever go home?"

"It doesn't seem like it does it, Andy?"

"Goodnight, Scully."

"Goodnight, Malone."

Andy walked the three blocks to his car. He parked away from the station so he didn't have to feed the meter. Besides, he liked to get the exercise if he was behind the desk a lot. That hadn't happened much lately! It was real dark and the street lights didn't seem to be lighting up the roads much tonight. A car went by him and the driver threw a cigarette butt out the window. Andy hated that! Then he saw it- the Caddie! He quickly ran the last one hundred yards to his car and pushed the snow that had fallen off the windows. But it was too late. They were so far gone he'd never catch them. He couldn't drive too well with the cast! Where were they going now?

Tony drove past Ned's front door and around the block casing the place. He wanted to make sure there was no one around. He didn't see a thing. Pulling into the alley, he let Ned out and he hobbled up to the back door and went in with Hal. Due to the snow, which Ned had not been around to shovel, the screen door would only open enough to squeeze past it and get the back door open. The place was cold and Ned tried to turn on the lights. He was surprised when they came on. He went over to the thermostat and saw it was set on low. Max! He must have kept up on it for him. Neighbors! Someday he'd have to thank him. "Don't turn on any more lights," said Hal, "just get the stuff you want and let's get out of here!"

Ned went to his bedroom closet and got his suitcase. He threw some of his clothes in and asked Hal, "What kind of weather should I pack for?"

Smiling and laughing Hal said, "I think it will be winter for a while." He took that to mean more of the same. When he got all he needed and Hal wasn't watching, he went over to the table and took a hundred dollars out of his pocket. He wrote on it "Max, hello from Ned" and set it under a can of beans on the table. Man the place was dusty! They walked out and locked the door.

Sven stepped up to take the ball from the rack. He was glad that he had a chance to play in this last tournament of the year. They usually didn't bowl on Fridays. So, it seemed odd to him. Enough so, that it seemed out of sorts and threw out his rhythm. The rest of the team seemed that way, too. They weren't doing so well. But Sven knew it wasn't just that. It was all the deaths and the fire. That had taken a toll on the moral of the team. They just didn't have it in them to play to win. But one thing about them, they were a team, and as brothers in Christ they loved being around one another. Pastor Wenck said to the group after about three frames, "OK men, I know it's been tough lately, but when the going gets tough the tough get going. Let's bowl like we mean it!"

"You betcha, Pastor!" Sven said.

The rest of the guys said, "Yahoo! Yeah, Yeah!"

Tony drove past St. Bernard's and Ned saw the cars. He wondered who was bowling that night. If he did, he could pick the winner! He chuckled to himself. "What?" Hal asked.

"Oh, nothing," Ned replied.

"No, really. What?" Hal insisted.

"I was just wondering who was bowling tonight," said Ned.

"Wanna see, Ned?"

"Really, Hal?"

"Yeah, but from the back and I ain't goin in there."

"Thanks, Hal!"

Tony stopped and opened the door for Ned. He got out and wobbled up to the door. Looking to see if there was anyone going in or out, he stepped in. No one noticed him and he went over by the coat room. It lent for a bit of safety there, as it was darker and had two posts to block the view. The girl that usually took the coats when they opened, was now working the concession stand. He stood by the front post and took a look over at the lanes. He saw the Lutherans and the FOP teams. The Eagles and Mason's were next on the board. When he saw Pastor Wenck, he had an idea. He took a fifty and wrote a note on the bill, "Hello, from Ned" and placed it in the pastor's pocket. Ned didn't want to arouse any suspicions, so he thought he had better get back to the car. Besides, he really didn't want to leave Hal now or even get him in trouble for that matter. No, he wanted to complete his plan first, so he dare not be seen or get caught. As he walked out the door, he looked back to see the score, the Lutherans were only 3 pins behind. "Well. I guess they'll pull it out. Good for them!"

When Ned got back in the car the guys were just sitting there listening to the radio. There had been a bulletin on WCCO about an explosion in White Bear. Ned got in and they were talking about it wondering who it could have been. "Sounds like a bad way to die, Boss," said Tony, "in a fireball like that." Ned didn't think anything about it. He *knew*.

Malone got two calls in the morning. The first was from Pastor Wenck. "Andy, I found something strange in my coat pocket when I got home from bowling last night."

"And what was that, Pastor?"

"When I stuffed my gloves back in there, I found a fifty dollar bill. On it was written, "Hello, from Ned.""

"What?!" replied the stunned cop.

"What do you make of that?"

"I don't know. I doubt someone would do that for fun. Fifty bucks to some is a lot of money."

"Do you think he was there at St. Bernard's?"

"I wouldn't put it past that Howard to have been there, too. But why would he allow Ned to go in?"

"It's all a mystery to me. I'll follow up on it, Pastor. I guess keep this money as a donation to the plate."

"Very well. I'll talk to you soon, Andy."

As soon as Malone hung up the phone it rang again. "Officer Malone, this is Max Scheming. I went over to Ned's to check on the place and you'll never guess what I found on the table under a can of beans."

Being a wise guy Andy replied, "A fifty dollar bill that says, "Hello, from Ned.""

Stunned, Max said, "No, it was a hundred. What do you want me to do with it?"

Malone chuckled and said, "Well, it's obvious he wanted you to have it. Maybe he figured you've been taking care of him, so he'd take care of you."

"You mean he was here?"

"Looks like it! Thanks for letting me know, Max."

"I'll keep a better eye on the place, Andy."

Malone hung up the phone when Commissioner Barfuss walked in. "How's it going, Malone?" asked the top cop. Andy stood and saluted. "No need for that. Sit down. I heard you had some kind of gang activity going on out here. Want to tell me about it?"

"Well Sir, a small time bookie was closed up last night, but I've found out that some of the more respected people in town have decided to make a little extra money on the side, if you know what I mean. It seems a mob boss from Chicago came in and nabbed a local baker who it is reported to be able to pick sports scores and is wandering all over the country just out of our reach with him. We'll catch up and put it all together. But it looks like we have the fire and some of the murders that revolve around the case solved."

"Good, Malone. Good work."

"Thank you, Sir." The Commissioner walked toward the Captain's door and went in. Andy wondered where Hal had taken Ned now.

Ned had fallen asleep after he got into the car. When he woke up it was still dark and he saw from the signs they were not going south this time, they were going west! The last mileage sign said,

"Billings- 150 miles." He didn't think much of it. Just figured it was another of Hal's tricks to throw off the cops. In reality it was a trick to throw off Ned! What Ned didn't know is that Hal had talked to his man on the inside down at the station. Hal knew all about Peters and now that the rat had sung, he was a dead man. Nothing Hal hated more than a squealer! So Hal decided to take Ned and drop him off at another old Army buddies house in Montana, Jim Rogers. He lived in Red Lodge and used to know Thomas Carroll. Hal figured he could get to know Ned, too.

When they pulled into town it had just warmed up. The Chinook wind had blown all the snow off the streets and it was in the 50's. Yet all around in the mountains, there was at least four feet of snow on the ground. Getting out of the car the three men went into the Red Lodge Café. There were stuffed animals all over the walls. Ned had never seen the head of a Buffalo before. And when he read the menu and saw he could get a buffalo burger, well, he was amazed. They were tired, but more than that they were hungry. They all ordered and the waitress brought them all some water. She bent over and Hal put his hand on her leg. She looked at him and smiled but said, "I'm sorry honey, but that isn't on the menu."

"Where's the best place to stay in town?"

"The Hotel is back a block that way," and she pointed the direction that they had come from. She walked to the back room.

Ned took a look around the room and saw mostly men with their cowboy hats and boots on. A couple guys looked like farmers and their wives looked just as any typical farm wife would- tough. The front door opened and the Sheriff walked in. The three of them looked down and turned their eyes away. It was obvious to all that the three were not from around there. It being winter made it even more obvious, because if it were summer they would have blended in with the tourists. But not now, not in winter, and even their Caddie with Illinois plates would stick out like a sore thumb. The cop walked past them without making any indication he noticed them.

The waitress brought their food and the men dug in. Tony was happy to see the huge portions. "This looks good," said the big Italian.

With juice coming from the corner of his mouth Ned said, "And this buffalo burger tastes great!"

The cop got up and walked over to the bar on the other side of the café. Hal breathed a sigh of relief and said, "You don't have to hurry boys, but when we're done, we better get over to the hotel."

When Hal went up to the register to pay the check the waitress came over to him. She slipped him a note and said, "Thanks Honey. Come again!" Hal looked around and saw that no one was paying attention. Tony smiled and held the door open for Ned as they walked back out onto Main Street. They got into the car and started back down toward the Hotel. Hal opened the note and it read, "Don't worry about the cops, Jim took care of it. Hope to see you soon!"

He smiled and said, "Looks like we are in for a smooth ride here boys."

"It's about time, Boss!" said Tony.

Ned just nodded in agreement and wondered what the note had said.

When they registered at the front desk the clerk handed them two keys, one for Hal and one for Tony and Ned. Stopping at room 200, Hal said, "I'm going to go to bed boys. I'll see you in the morning."

"OK, Boss," replied Tony and Hal threw him the key to their room. "Some shut-eye sounds pretty good about now," said Tony and they made their way down the hall toward 214. Tony went in first. Ned picked up his bag and dropped his cane on the floor. Just then a guy came by and he stopped and picked it up for him. Handing it to him he winked and said, "Here you go, Ned."

"Thank you," replied a surprised Ned. The man just kept on going and Ned saw he stopped at Hals' room and knocked. Ned waited long enough for the stranger to go in. Then he followed

Tony into 214 wondering who this guy was, how he knew him, and why he looked familiar to him.

Chapter Twenty-Eight- Easter in The Big Sky

Andy sat at his desk looking out the window. It had been a long winter, but now spring was in the air. He could see the walls of Concordia Lutheran going up and the workmen taking a break on the front stairs. He'd talked to Pastor Wenck the other day and he said that Sven had given the forty-eight grand to the church to rebuild. All this after the detectives had determined they could find that there was no link to it being stolen from anyone or a crime other than Olaf's death. Sven just didn't feel right about keeping it and he thought Olaf would have wanted it this way. Scully walked up to Andy and asked, "What ya thinkin, Andy?"

"Just watching how God can bring good from a bad deal."

"Oh. Yeah. I see what ya mean. How's Sven doin these days?"

"Better. He hired the new help after Olga died and the rest of his family has been around lately. And winning the bowling championships a couple months ago helped his ego too. He's such a nice guy."

"Have you picked up the trail on Ned?"

"No. Not a thing. And that worries me. Nothing on any of them."

Ned woke to the sound of a rooster. Hal had left him in the care of Jim. After he had seen him at the Hotel that night, Ned finally remembered him. They had all served Uncle Sam in the same unit. Now, living on the ranch west of Luther, he was actually quite satisfied. Ned did all the cooking. Actually, he was the chief cook and bottle washer. He had twenty people to take care of and it reminded him of his days in the service. The cowhands appreciated the good food, which was a big change for them, because Jim's wife Sandy was a better calver than a cook, and Ned felt like he was contributing. And of course, he still did his "job" for Hal and the money kept rolling in. Ned had been placing a few bets of his own and his bank account had grown the past couple of months. He now had over five hundred grand in his account. Hal knew all this, but he didn't care. Even though he had paid for Ned, his investment had been a pittance of what he had made off Ned's "gift."

Ned took another loaf of bread out of the oven. It went well with the bacon and eggs he had retrieved from the hen house. He meant to tell Frank that he noticed a coyote had been digging under the fence again. Ned was afraid he'd get through next time. Jim came in from the barn and took off his boots by the door. "Man, the rain sure makes it hard to work this time of year." The rest of the hands followed him in and they all sat down to eat.

"We're sure glad you came along when you did, Ned," said Clive the lanky hand from Denver way.

"Yeah," joined in Sammy who was just as lean and tough, "you saved our lives!"

Laughing, they all dug in and Sandy just slapped Sammy's shoulder knowing that this dig was aimed at her.

Ned told Frank about the coyote after the rest of the crew went out to mend fences after the long winter. It seemed like the snow would never go away. The worst part is that the snow fences didn't work as usual. It all blew the other direction and a lot of the barbed wire sections had the most snow. And to the men, it seemed to have taken its toll on the mending they had done last year. Frank said he'd "take care" of the pesky coyote.

Ned sat down to finally have breakfast himself. Sandy sat down to talk to him. "Say Ned," she asked, "have you thought about going to town with us for the Easter services?"

"Easter services?" asked a curious Ned.

"Yes. Even though most of the crew doesn't seem like they're too religious, it is one of the times of year I can get them into church. That and Christmas."

Ned remembered Christmas in Florida. The angel incident seemed just like a far off dream to him. It seemed like eons ago. Ned replied, "I'd very much like that. Are you Catholic or ?" Leaving his question opened ended, he fished for a denomination.

“We’re Lutheran. We plan on going to service when Pastor Hovland comes from Absarokee in the afternoon. Are you Lutheran?”

“No, I’m Catholic, but I will come with you. I appreciate the invitation.” Ned got up and took his plate to the sink and started the dishes.

Sandy said, “See you later, Ned. I’ve got to check on the herd.”

“OK, Sandy, see you later.” Looking out the kitchen window, Ned watched her get on her horse and ride out to the south forty where the herd was. He thought about Malachi again and wondered if he would make another appearance this Easter.

In Minnesota, Sven took some more hot cross buns out of the oven and handed them to Ava. He started to put another batch in when the phone rang. “Heidi, would you get da phone?” Heidi left the register and came back to the phone hanging on the wall in the back room. She usually picked up the extension in the front by the register, but somehow it had broken last week. It made it hard to take orders for her. “Hallo, Tschida’s bakery,” she chimed.

“This is Officer Malone. Could I talk to Sven please?” Suddenly, out of the corner of her eye Heidi caught it, a fire beside the ovens! She dropped the phone and screamed,

“FIRE, FIRE!”

Andy heard all the commotion and yelled back into the phone, “Heidi, what’s going on??!” He could hear Sven yelling something about the extinguisher and the sound of it being used on the fire. “Whosshhh. Whoosshhhh,” it went.

Sven picked up the phone. “Andy is dat you?”

“Yes, Sven. Is everything alright?”

“Ya, sure. But if it not be for you, and Heidi comin into da back room to answer da phone, we be a burnt piece of toast, don’t ya know!”

“Do you want the fire department to come?”

"No. We have it under control. Why did you call, Andy?"

"It doesn't matter now. I'll call back later."

Sven hung up the phone and went back to cleaning up the mess and assessing the damage. It wasn't bad. It just got some of the paper and bags. He had left them there and had not had time to put them on the shelf were they belonged. It was his own fault. If it had not been for Malone's call and the broken phone up front, the place would have burned down! The phone rang. This time it rang up front! Sven looked at Heidi. She picked it up and asked, "Tschida's Bakery?"

"I'd like to order some poppy seed bread. This is Pam Pofal ."

"Oh ya, sure, we made them today, Pam. How would many you like?"

Sven wondered what it all meant. He didn't feel like it was just luck. The angel looking on just smiled and took a smell of the hot cross buns.

On Easter Day in Luther, the cowboys all got into the trucks, and Jim and Sandy put Ned into the car. It was a twenty-five mile ride into town to go to First Lutheran. The congregation had been struggling, but there was still a small group of worshipers that Pastor Hovland served coming from Absarokee once a month. Ned was in good spirits as they drove into town. It had been a while since he'd been there.

They pulled up to the front door and let Ned out. Sandy helped him up the steps and Pastor Hovland was there to greet the worshipers. "Good morning, Sandy! He is Risen!"

"He is risen indeed!" she responded.

"Nice to have you here today, Sandy, and who is this gentleman with you?"

"This is Ned. A friend of Jim's. They served in the war together in France."

"The great war! Pleased to meet you, Ned."

"Nice to meet you too, Pastor."

The rest of the group came in and Pastor Hovland greeted them in the same manner as Sandy and Ned. Ned figured it had to be a Lutheran thing. They went in to take their seats. It looked to Ned like everyone had their own special place to sit- much like a pecking order. He didn't say anything and looked at the order of service the usher handed him when he went in. "Hmmm", he muttered, "looks like mass."

The pastor began the service. By now the light of the morning sky was coming into the side windows. The stained glass had scenes from the bible on each of them and the glass shown brilliantly with the sun. "Today, this first day of April, we keep in our prayers our valiant soldiers all over the world, praying for their safe return." As Pastor Hovland began to pray, the bells in the old Finnish church they were in, began to chime. Ever so slowly at first and the congregation did not seem to make much of it. Then faster and faster the bells rang out, and louder and louder they became. The preacher turned around to inquire of the elder at the back of the room. The elder looked up the tower to see who was ringing the bells, but found no one there and the bells were ringing themselves! Finally leaving the altar, Pastor Hovland hurriedly went to see about the ringing himself. Making his way to the narthex he said, "What are you doing Ewald? Why are you ringing the bells?"

"But Pastor," Ewald said, *"no one is ringing the bells!"* In disbelief he looked for himself and sure enough, there was no one there! There was no wind, just the bells ringing as fast and loud as they could be rung. By now the whole of the congregation was at the entrance of the church looking at the entire spectacle.

Ned sat in his pew looking at the stained glass of the angel. The angel had seemed to come to life. He was the only one who noticed it as the bells rang and the people focused their attention to them. Malachi began to speak to Ned. "Behold Ned, the army of men shall return from Europe on May the 7th." Suddenly the bells just stopped and the bright light coming in from the sun disappeared. The angel was gone.

Pastor Hovland came back to the front of the church totally distraught. He said, “Brothers and sisters, let us continue in the heavenly worship begun here this day by angels from above!” Little did he know how right he was! Ned was glad the war would be over soon! He sang with the choir the hymn, “Praise to the Lord!”

Hal and Tony took a cab to the brunch after mass. It was nice to be home in Chicago for a change. They decided at the last minute to go to church on Easter. Besides, the last time they went with Ned at Christmas, they were wondering if anything weird would happen again without him there. When they left the church, they were relieved that it was just a normal Easter with the priest asking everyone where they had been for so long.

The brunch was a new thing that some guy on the lake had come up with. Kind of like a ‘breakfast smorgasbord’, thought Tony. When they got there, the place was packed. “Looks like this brunch thing is taking off,” said Tony to Hal.

“Yeah, hope it’s as good as it looks.”

When they took their seats at the table, they wondered what was going on in the back of the room. It looked like a large group that was taking up three tables. The group was made up of about four of five families- all speaking Italian. Then Tony recognized a couple of the guys. They were mobsters from the other side of town with their families. Hal didn’t mind them coming over to his side of the turf. Not for this kind of stuff. Besides, he’d been making a lot of money off of them lately! One of the goons noticed Tony and waved. Tony waved back and said, “Hey Pisano!”

The waitress came and took their drink orders and the men got up to go through the food line. Tony couldn’t believe the amount of food. Hal was pleased about its quality. When they got back to their chairs, someone from the other side began to act angrily. They could hear them say, “I don’t care if they place all their bets right! They’re cheats and I want them dead!”

With that Tony sprang up in front of Hal. Just in time too, because the thug pulled out a gun and took a shot at Hal. The bullet grazed Tony's arm. Hal took out his gun and shot the guy right in the side of his face. Everyone in the place hit the floor. Hal and Tony threw a couple of tables in the way, took a couple of more shots, and made their way to the door of the kitchen. "What the heck was that all about?" screamed Hal to Tony.

As they ran out of the back and towards a cab Tony screamed back, "I don't know, but I think they have a war on their hands!"

As they jumped in a cab Hal said, "I don't know, Tony. I don't have the manpower for that. I think we've been in town long enough. Let's scram."

In St. Paul, Pastor Wenck finished up his Easter service and was saying hello to everyone as they left. He was glad they ALL had come. He was glad that finally his flock would be back in their own building again soon. If anything, the fire had drawn them together. Besides, it was a burden on the people at St. Bernard's to let them worship there each Sunday afternoon. The builder had let him know that it would be about four more months and they could start having services again at Concordia, but that they would not be done with all the finishing touches. Carl was happy with that! And so was the congregation.

Father McCarthy walked up to him just as Carl was closing the door. "Hello, Richard. Glad to see you. I just wanted to let you know that we will most likely be into our new building in four months or so, God willing."

"That's such good news!" responded the cleric.

"Indeed," said Carl, "and if you or your congregation ever needs anything, please don't hesitate to ask. My flock will be glad to help."

"As a matter of fact," replied Father McCarthy, "there is a little thing I'd like to talk to you about."

"And that is?"

"I think it would bring our people closer together and…"

Carl cut him off. "What *is* it, Richard?"

"We have a problem with the convent and I heard you have a lot of tradesmen. Do you think they could help?"

"Indeed! We certainly can!"

When the Godfather heard about the scuffle in Chicago on Easter Day he was eating at the Stork Club and he was furious. "It all started with the Baker. I want you to get him!"

"But we don't know where he is. Hal doesn't have him with him. He just fell off the face of the earth!"

"I don't care! Find him! And while you're at it, get rid of Howard, too!"

Hal called Ned to ask him about a bet. It was to be, "The Bet", he had been waiting for. "Ned, I'd like you to tell me who is going to win tonight in Florida. The Yanks or Red Sox?"

Ned thought about it for a second and said, "How about the date for the end of the war?"

"Really? Would that work? It's not a game. But that's even better! What is it?"

"May 7th."

"Thanks, Ned." Hal placed the bet before he left his room. He bet all he had- *one million dollars!* The bookie on the other end thought he was kidding. Hal got upset with him. "Listen to me," he said, "do I ever kid?"

"No, Boss. But if you win, it will be the biggest payout the mob has ever had to make! The odds are 125 to 1!!!"

"Just place the bet."

"OK. OK." The guy hung up.

When Hal and Tony left Chicago, they didn't notice the Buick following them. They made their way toward Florida to see Diego. What they didn't know is that Diego already had company.

Andy heard all about it on the news. Something that big always makes the national news. Just think- a gun fight at a restaurant on Easter Day! Sounded like something Hal Howard would get into! He hoped it led to something on Ned....

Chapter Twenty-Nine- Ned makes a purchase

It was already Friday night after Easter. Ned took some of the trout and put it in the colossal sized iron skillet that hung from the wall on a horse shoe. One of the men had taken the time to catch a mess from the creek. There must have been eighty or so brook trout for Ned to cook. "Just might be enough to feed the whole gang," Ned said to himself.

The men started to file in one-by-one. Each of them commented on how good the trout smelled and on how hard the day was. They were all beat- dead tired. When Jim came in he said, "I know it's been tough here lately boys, so tomorrow we go into town for a little R&R!"

"Yahoo! Thanks boss!" they replied.

Tony stopped at a Shell station for gas and a pack of cigarettes. Hal went to the rest room. Digging his comb out of his pocket, Tony looked in the side mirror and ran it thru his hair. It was then that he noticed the Buick. It had stopped around the corner and the guy was watching every move he made. Tony put the nozzle back on the pump, not waiting for the attendant. He went in to pay. "Boss, there's a guy sittin in a Buick around the corner."

Trusting his man, Hal said, "Just do what you think. I'm only in the back seat." Tony paid for the gas, his cigarettes, and headed to the car. Hal couldn't help it and bought a bottle of Coke.

When they got in, Tony said, "Hold on Boss, because here we go!" When Tony got onto the road he hit the gas and the car lurched forward. Hal had to grab hold of the bottle and almost spilled it when the car lunged forward. There was no catching Tony. The Buick just didn't have it in it and all Hal saw was a small dot in the rear view mirror. Tony was amazing! Hal took a swig of Coke and smiled.

When Tony drove up to the door in Key West, he had a bad feeling. If Tony had a bad feeling he was usually right. Acting on his instinct he drove right on through and parked on the side street. Hal noticed all this and asked, "Got a hunch, Tony?"

"Sure do, Boss."

"Well check it out, and come and let me know." Tony got out and walked around the back of the house. Looking through the porch window he saw Diego working on house cleaning like normal. But he noticed him talking to someone with his hands. Tony moved around to the side and looked in that window. There he saw another man. This one he also recognized. It was the same guy that had come to St. Paul and tried to take Ned for the Godfather! Beside him was "Lefty" from Chicago, too. Tony knew he had trouble! He made his way back to the car, careful to not be seen. "It's that punk from New York City , Hal!"

"Great! The Godfather must have heard about the Easter thing and is out to get us. Let's get out of here."

"But boss, we're running out of places to go!"

"Not yet Tony. I got an ace up my sleeve." And so he did!

Back in Montana, Ned rode into town with Sandy and they stopped across the street from the café. And then he saw it! A bakery next door was for sale! It was what he always wanted- his *own* bakery. He got visibly excited and Sandy knew it. She said, "It's been for sale for a while. Want to go in?"

"Yes!"

Ned walked out into the street and almost got hit by a Packard. The horns blared out and frightened him. He dropped his cane. Sandy bent over and picked it up for him. Smiling, she asked, "Are you OK?"

"Yeah. I guess I just got excited."

They walked in the door and Ned looked around. It needed some work and a little updating, but it would work. All he would need is a little help. He asked the man behind the counter if he was the owner. "No, he's in the back room."

"How many people work here?"

The counter man said reservedly, “There are three of us, why?”

“Oh nothing. Could I see the boss?”

The guy went into the back and came out with a tall light haired man of obvious Nordic decent. “Ya, could I help you?”

“I’m Ned Oelker. I’m interested in buying your bakery. Is it still for sale?”

The baker shook his head up and down hurriedly. “Ya, for sure! I just take it off the market mit da realtor. His sign just still in da vindow. But I sell to you today!”

“Let’s talk,” said Ned.

All of this time, Malone was still looking for Ned. Then, Malone got a message from Detective Holmstrom. Scully wrote, “Holmstrom says he has information about Hal Howard from the Peter’s case. Call him.” He picked up the phone and dialed. When someone answered he asked, “Is Holmstrom in?”

Not answering him, he heard a guy on the other end yell, “Holmstrom, phone.” The guy set it down hard and Holmstrom came on a few seconds later.

“Holmstrom,” he said.

“This is Malone. I heard you got some more info.”

“Oh, yeah. It looks like he’s got another place. You’re not going to believe where it is- Niagara Falls.”

“Really?”

“Yup.”

“OK. Thanks Holmstrom.”

Andy picked up the phone again and called a friend in Canada on the other side from Niagara. “Pierre, this is Andy Malone.”

“Andy my friend! Are you in town?”

“No Pierre, I am in St.Paul. I have a favor to ask of you. Have you ever heard of Hal Howard?”

"Oh yes. He's a small time mafia boss. He has a place across ze river. Why do you want him?"

"He kidnapped a baker here. See if he comes around will ya?"

"I'll have to do it off the record on my own time!"

"You're a pal. Thanks Pierre!"

"Au revoir, Andy."

Meanwhile, Ned called First National bank in St. Paul and got the teller he had been working with all this time. "Patsy, this is Ned Oelker, how are you?"

"Oh just fine, Ned. What can I do for you?"

"I need to have you send me a wire transfer to the Red Lodge, Montana branch of the First National Bank."

"In what amount?"

"Twenty-five thousand dollars."

"To whose attention do I make it?"

"VP, Michael Fulbright. Got it?"

"Got it."

"Oh, and by the way, I'll be moving some of my account to the same bank soon. Thanks, Patsy."

"OK. Bye, Ned."

Ned hung up and said to Sandy, "It looks like I'll soon own a bakery!"

On a hunch, the Minnesota cop went over to see Max and snoop around Ned's house. When he answered the door he said to Andy, "Oh just go on in, Andy. The front door is open. I was just there."

"Why did ya leave the door open?"

"It stinks and I was airing it out." Andy shook his head and went into the house. All the drapes were pulled shut. He opened the front room shade and light poured in, and then was able to take a look around. The place was getting pretty dirty. Not from use, but from no one being around. He looked at the garbage can and figured out why it stunk in there, so he took the can and opened the back door and set it on the stoop. He wondered why there was a ridge of snow packed up where the screen door stopped. Then he knew that Ned had come in the back. No one else had gone in or out that way. Not even Max. He looked around and saw the dresser drawers open and some more of Ned's things gone. He figured Ned must have wanted some of his stuff if he had planned on being away for a long period of time. "That's it," he said out loud, "he's not planning on coming back!" What he couldn't figure out was-why?

The rest of the cowboys had gone over to the Senate Bar to have a drink or two. Then one of them said, "Hey- lets go over to Bear Creek!"

Sammy said, "Naw, it's too rough over there. Those miners are crazy!"

"So what? Let's go!"

"You guys can, but I'm stayin here."

"Suit yourself!" Clive and a few of the guys walked out and got in the pickup.

Sammy stayed with a couple of the others. He said, "Hope we don't have to go bail them out like last time."

Jim came in the bar just then. Sandy and Ned were right behind him. "Where's Clive and the rest?" he asked.

Sammy said, "Those idiots went over to Bear Creek."

Jim turned to Sandy. She said, "You know what that means don't you?"

"Yeah. We may as well go over to the jail right now and wait."

"I'll take Ned home and come back to get you, OK?"

Jim said, "You'll know where I'll be!"

Sandy drove Ned back to the ranch. There was no need to say anything. Both of them knowing full well what the situation was. Ned was tired. Sandy knew it had been a long day for him. When she pulled up to the door Ned asked, "Do you mind if I call Hal on the phone while you're gone?"

"Do I mind? He's paying for it! Go ahead! Good night, Ned. Don't wait up."

"Good night, Sandy." Ned got out and hobbled up to the door. Jim's blue healer "Moon" came up to him and licked his hand. When he got in, the phone rang their party line ring, four shorts. Ned answered, "Hello?"

"Why, hello Ned! How are you buddy?"

"Hal! I was just going to call you!"

"How were you going to do that? You don't know where I am!"

"Aren't you in Chicago?"

"No. Niagara Falls."

"Niagara Falls? Why there?"

"It's too complicated. Ned, where's Jim?"

"He's in town waiting to bail some of the hands out of jail."

"What did they get into this time?"

"Bear Creek."

"Oh. That."

"Yeah. Say Hal, I got something to tell you."

"What's that, Ned?"

"I bought a bakery today."

"You what?"

"I bought a bakery today."

"I heard you the first time. Why did you do that? You have plenty of money. You can retire, Ned."

"I know, but it's what I love and it's something I always wanted to have- my own bakery."

"In Red Lodge, Montana?"

"It's perfect Hal. I"ll have to do a little remodeling, but I have the help and the money."

"OK. But you'll have to wait until I release you from your job with me."

"Hal, I can do that part time and still do this."

"Yeah. You're right. No one's gotta know."

"That's right. I take possession in a week. I hope the guys don't get too upset having to eat Sandy's cooking again."

Hal laughed. "Tell Jim to call me when he gets home."

"Good night, Hal."

"Good night, Ned." They both hung up. Hal turned to Tony and said, "It looks like I just lost an employee."

Tony looked out the window. He thought he saw someone casing the place. Niagara Falls was even colder than St. Paul and Chicago. He saw the breath of someone standing behind a post on the sidewalk. Tony went out the back door and came up behind the man. He grabbed him by the arm and put him in an arm lock. "What are you doing here?" said Tony to the intruder.

In a French accent the man said, "Nothing, just grabbing a smoke."

"Get out of here and don't come back." Tony let the man go and gave him a shove toward the street. Pierre slid along the sidewalk and after gaining his balance ran as fast as he could away from Tony.

Pierre called Andy when he got back to the office. “He’s there.”

“Who’s there? Hal?”

“Yes my friend, Hal and a big goon. He caught me by the arm last night and almost broke it. He’s one big man.”

“That would be Tony. And he is one big man. Thanks, Pierre. I owe you one.”

“Oui, you do.”

Back inside, Tony said to Hal, “It was just some Canadian out for a walk.”

“I wonder what’s keeping Jim from calling. He should be in by now.”

“Maybe the guys got into more trouble than he thought!” Hal Laughed and said, “So what else is new? Those cowboys are always a pain in the butt.”

“What did you want to tell him, Boss?”

“That he should let Ned go so he can run his new bakery. And, because it’s getting too hot here, that we are moving out of the country.”

“We’re what? But Boss, I want to go to Las Vegas!”

“Are you crazy? Jackie and Moe ain’t thinkin. They’ll both be ruined and in jail, or dead. Trust me. We’re taking our money and moving to Argentina via- Canada.”

“Too hot, huh? I’d say it’s pretty cold out there!” They both laughed and took a drink of a hot toddy. “Besides, after the bet I just placed, we won’t have to ever worry about anything ever again.”

In St. Paul, Andy knew he had to act fast if he was going to catch Hal this time. The guy just moved around too fast! He called the Falls police. “Niagara Falls Police Department,” the voice said on the other side of the line.

"This is Officer Andy Malone of the St. Paul, Minnesota Police Department. I have a tip that a wanted mafia boss is there in town and is hiding. Do you have anyone that can go out and apprehend the man and his bodyguard?"

"I'll connect you to Detective Hale."

"Detective Hale. How can I help you?"

Andy went through the whole story this time. Hale was excited and very helpful. "I'll get some backup and get out there right away, Andy," he said. "It's not often us cops up here get anyone of this importance."

"Be careful. The big guy can punch!"

When Hale and the black and whites got to Hal's place they watched it happen. It was hard to miss! Suddenly, as they drove up to the cottage, it just blew up in front of them! The whole entire house went flying past them like a million toothpicks! There wasn't even a fire. Thank goodness they had not gotten out of the car. When they did, a 2x4 was stuck in the grill of the squad car. They walked up to the house and peered in. Nothing to find here; no car either. Whoever was in there was surely dead! Hale called Andy.

Scully took the call. "Sure Detective, I'll tell him."

When Andy got back to his desk Scully broke the bad news. "Looks like your search for Hal Howard is over. The mob blew him up." That left Andy with nothing. The Godfather wasn't happy either!

Max heard the doorbell. A telegraph boy was on the doorstep. "I have a telegram for Max Scheming."

"I'm Max. I'll take it." He gave the boy a quarter and closed the door. He was afraid to open it. So many people had been getting bad news in the war and he knew he was not immune. He had relatives in Europe and he knew all about Hitler. He let it sit on the table for about an hour. Finally, he got up the nerve to open it. Slowly he read the first line. "Alive and well. Stop. Expect package from bank. Stop. Be home from bakery soon. Stop. Don't expect rye. Stop. Ned." Max fainted.

When he woke he called Tschida's. "Sven, have you seen Ned?"

Wondering what prompted the question Sven replied, "No. Are you alright, Max?"

"I got a telegram from Ned."

"You vat? You got a telegram von Ned? Ver is he?"

"I don't know. It's kind of cryptic. Said he was coming home from the bakery. That's why I called you."

"He's not here. By gosh, by golly, this is something."

"Well thanks, Sven. I'm going to call Officer Malone."

"Gud idea, Max."

Chapter Thirty- Ned's first flight

Ned packed his bag and asked Sandy for a ride into town. "When does the bus for Billings come in?"

"It comes in every day about two," she said.

"Good. That'll give me time to go see a couple of people before I leave." Before they left the hands all came in and said goodbye to Ned.

Sammy said, "Sorry to see you go Ned. You're the best cook we ever had!"

"Come in to the bakery and see me. You can eat as much as you pay for!" They both laughed and Sammy slapped Ned on the back as he walked out.

Sandy asked, "Ready to go Ned?"

"Yup."

Sandy dropped Ned off at the curb in front of the bank. She waved goodbye and drove off. Ned watched her as she went down the street and he turned to go into the bank. He walked in and seeing a familiar face from church on Easter in the front said, "My name is Ned Oelker. I'd like to see the manager."

"How are you today? My name is Frieda. What may I ask is it about, Mr. Oelker?" she asked.

"Please call me Ned. It's about a new account," Ned replied.

Overhearing the banter a man came up to them and said, "I can help you with that, my name is Michael Fulbright. It's nice to finally meet you. Please sit down, Mr. Oelker."

"Thank you. May I call you Michael?"

"Please, call me Mike. No need to be so formal around here. How much would you like to deposit, Ned?"

"I'm going to have you call my bank in Minnesota. The woman in charge of my account is named Patsy. I intend to transfer four hundred thousand dollars."

The VP dropped his pen. "Did you say four hundred thousand dollars?"

"Yes. But, I want this kept strictly confidential. I don't want the community to know my business. Except for the bakery that is!" The men both chuckled. When he left he stopped at Frieda's desk once again. "I hope you don't think this too forward, but may I call on you sometime Frieda?"

"Yes, but I'll see you in church again soon, won't I?"

"Yes, you will!" Ned walked out of the bank having accomplished more than he thought he would!

After he finished at the bank, he went in to see the bakery once more. He wanted to firm up the fact that the people who worked for Helmut would stay on and work for him after the sale. When Ned walked in, the guy at the counter, the same one that was in there the other day, announced to the entire bakery, "The new boss is here!"

Helmut came out of the back room wiping the flour from his hands. "Hallo, Ned. So nice to see you. Vat can we help you mit?"

"I'd like to see if all the employees would consider staying on with me after I take over the bakery."

"Funny you should ask! Ve all talked about that and they would be honored to stay on." They all came out and Helmut introduced them. Ned was pleased.

The bus ride was supposed to be a short one hour ride with only one stop in Rockvale. Ned was sitting next to the window until they got to that first stop. They had to wait for a passenger that was on the phone, which made some of them antsy. A serviceman got on and sat down next to him, dropping his duffle bag into the aisle. Looking at his uniform Ned said, "Hello my name is Ned. Are you going back Sergeant?"

"Yes, Sir," responded the soldier.

"Where to this time?"

"Wherever they send me."

"You won't have much action this time. The war in Europe will end on May 7th."

The soldier looked at him oddly and said, "From your lips to God's ears."

Ned asked, "Are you Jewish?"

"Why yes, how did you know?"

"My best friend is Jewish!" said Ned, and he began to tell him all about Max and his life in St. Paul. By the time they got off the bus Ned had a new friend. He said to the Sergeant as he got up to leave, "Thanks for your service to me and your country. Call on me at the Red Lodge Bakery when you get home."

"You got it, Ned!"

When he arrived at the airport in Billings, Ned was a little apprehensive about flying back to St. Paul. He inquired at the counter about a ticket. "And you say I can be there twice as fast as if I took the train?" He was tired of long rides!

"Faster than that," replied the clerk.

"And it only cost ten dollars more?"

"That's right."

"I'll take it."

Ned got on the plane and sat next to the window behind the wing.

The stewardess came to him and asked, "Have you ever flown before?"

"No. I can't say that I have."

"Well, don't worry. It may get a little rough at times. But, it's safe and we'll only have to stop one time to refuel." Ned nodded his head in affirmation of her explanation and looked out the window.

The plane started to fill up. A woman sat next to him and introduced herself. “I’m Margo. And you are?”

“Ned,” he replied.

“Ned, I’ve never known a Ned before. Now, I do.” They began to talk and it took his mind off the flight. By the time they got Bismark to refuel, he was all talked out. He wanted to take a nap. She excused herself to go to the restroom. He saw his chance to try to take a snooze. He placed his hat over his eyes and leaned against the window. When she got back the plane was ready to taxi out the runway for the trip to St. Paul. She didn’t have the heart to wake him, so she picked up a magazine and began to read. He glanced over and smiled. He fell asleep with the hum of the engines.

On the ground, the phone rang and Andy picked it up to hear an excited Max say, “I got a telegram from Ned!”

“You did? Where is he?”

“I don’t know. He didn’t say. But I know he’s coming home soon.”

“How do you know that?”

“Because, he said so.”

“Read me the telegram, Max.” So, Max read it for him.

“Hum,” said Andy, “coming home from the bakery. What could that mean? If he sends you anything else, especially from the bank, let me know right away.”

“You got it Andy.”

Andy called Western Union. “This is Officer Malone, St. Paul Police. A telegram was sent to Max Scheming on Rose Street today. Can you tell me the office of origin?”

The clerk said, “Sure. Give me a minute to look it up.” He came back and said, “It was sent from Billings, Montana.”

“Thanks.”

"You bet officer."

Andy finally knew where Ned was! He was on his way back to St. Paul!

Chapter Thirty-One- Ned Goes to Tschida's

Andy saw Pastor Wenck at Schiller's grocery. He moved his basket over so Mrs. Dahlquist could get by and the Pastor could speak to Andy. "How's the building project coming Pastor?" asked Andy.

"Just fine, Andy! If they keep going at this rate, we'll be in there by the Fourth of July!"

"That's great news!"

"I think I've figured out who your secret benefactor is."

"Who would that be?"

"I believe it is Ned Oelker."

"Ned? How? Why? He's not even a Lutheran! Do you know where he is?"

"Yes, I do. And I think he'll be here soon. If you see him will you call me?"

"Sure will, Andy. After I give him a big hug!"

Sven saw the back door to the bakery open and a cane come through it. Before anyone appeared he knew who it was. He dropped the dough he was working on and ran toward the door shouting, "NED!" The others heard him yell and came running to see what all the commotion was about. Ava recognized Ned, but Heidi had never met him.

"Hello Sven, how are you?" said Ned.

"No, my friend, how are you? Are you OK?"

"Just fine, Sven, just fine."

"Come. Sit down. Tell me all about everyting."

Ned sat on the stool he used to sit on, so he could keep working when his back got tired. "Well, let's just say this, I've seen a lot of America and I'm glad I live in a country like this!"

The front door opened and closed. Expecting someone to ring the counter bell Heidi went toward the front but was met by— Honey Malone, who heard the laughing and came back to see what it was all about. “Ned! I’m so glad to see you’re safe! My husband has been trying to find you for months.”

“Tell your husband I’m safe and sound.” As Honey went to the phone to call Andy, Ned told the group all about his “captivity”.

When the house blew up back in Niagara Falls, Tony and Hal were about a half a block away in the Caddie. Tony looked up to see a piece of roof go up about a block into the air. He laughed and said, “Looks like the Godfather did a good job rubbing us out Boss.”

“Sure did!” said Hal. And they laughed all the way to the Canadian border.

Andy got the call from Honey and went right over to the bakery. When he got there, a crowd had formed filling the entire place. Andy saw Ma Klein, Ben Egger, Bruce Katz, and even some of the gang from the Stahl House. There was laughing and talking about how Ned had come back unharmed. It was a miracle. When Andy pushed his way back to Ned, he breathed a sigh of relief. He looked OK. “Hello Ned. Glad to see you back!”

“Hello Andy!” Ned got up and went over to him and shook his hand. “Thank you so much for continuing the search for me all these past months, but what happened to your arm?”

“Long story,” Andy replied, “and I want to hear yours, too. Can you fill me in?”

“Sure, Andy, but can I come in tomorrow? I have some things to take care of.”

“Sure, Ned. Call me.”

Just then Max came in. He ran up to Ned and gave him a big hug. Ned just tolerated it and kept his head back and shook it back and forth and said, “Oy vay!”

"Thanks for sending me the papers to your house, Ned. I'm going to bring over my relatives from Europe."

"Don't mention it Max. You've been taking care of it all this time and you deserve it."

"Does that mean you not coming back to stay?" Sven asked.

"Yes, it does, Sven. It looks like you have a handle on the bakery now, with Thor, Ava, and Heidi, and to tell you the truth, I bought me my own bakery out west."

The crowd started to break up and they all wished Ned luck on his new venture. Ben Egger had waited around and was just standing there with a package in his hands. He came up to Ned and said. "It's nice to see you Ned. I brought this for you. They were from this fall on the Kinni."

It was a peace offering from Ben. Ned took the package of frozen trout from Ben and said, "Thanks Ben." They shook hands and Ben went toward the door.

As Sven was turning off the lights, a knock came on the bakery door. It was Pastor Wenck. Sven opened the door again and before he could say anything to him, Carl flew by him saying, "I just heard Ned was here. Ned, are you in the back?"

"Yes, Pastor. I'm here." When he turned the corner and saw Ned, he went up to him and gave him a hug. He reacted the same way with Carl as he did Max.

"Thank you so much for your generosity these past months. You don't know what it meant to the congregation. With your gifts and Sven's donation, we have put the church back on its feet."

Ned looked at Sven. Sven said, "Oh ya, you don't know. Olaf die and I give his money to da church. No big deal."

"You didn't know it, but I was at the funeral, Sven. I'm sorry about Olaf."

"Really? Me, too."

After this, the three men went to the Tin Cups for dinner. It was only then that Sven and Pastor where able to understand what had truly happened to Ned. They talked until past dark with Ned explaining everything, even his Angel. Pastor Wenck was intrigued about this. He said, “It looks like God was protecting you and all of us through this attack from Satan. Obviously, he was trying to take back the playing field to what it was like before they cleaned up St.Paul. And obviously, God is in control and He sent his Messenger to tell us. God truly changes hearts.”

When they finished up, Sven asked Ned to stay with him in Olaf’s old room. Ned said he’d like that, so they made their way toward the bakery. The moon was full and the street lights almost paled in comparison in their effect on the roadway. Along the way Sven asked, “Will you stay long Ned?”

“No, Sven. I have a new business to open and it won’t wait for me. I need to get back in the next couple of days.”

“I understand. Would you like to help me in da morning?”

“You bet, Sven! I can’t think of anything better!”

Ned didn’t have any trouble sleeping that night. In fact, he awoke on his old schedule, just in time to dress and go downstairs to get out the proofing boxes for Sven. “Good morning, Ned,” said Sven.

“Good morning, Sven,” said Ned as he put on his apron. It was just like old times.

Ava and the apprentice, Thor, came to the door and Sven let them in. “Oh what a nice surprise!” she exclaimed, “Good morning, Ned. You too, Sven!” She laughed. They all laughed.

The day went by quickly, none of them, not even Heidi, skipping a beat in the precision known as Tschida’s Bakery. As they wrapped up the last of their day, Sven asked Ned, “Vill you go home tomorrow?”

"Yes, I think so. I want to go see Suzie today. Then I'll pack and try to leave tomorrow."

"Vant to go to Como on the way? I'll see if ve can get a ride?"

"Yes, maybe we could con Father McCarthy into taking us? I'll call him, Sven."

Ned went to the back room to call his priest. The phone rang twice and he answered, "St. Bernard's Catholic Church. This is Father McCarthy."

"Hello, Father. This is Ned." Ned could have heard a pin drop. Obviously, the priest had not yet heard he was back.

"Ned? Really? That is you? When? How? Are you Ok?"

"Yes, Father. Yes! I got back yesterday. I'm surprised you haven't heard. The whole block is talking about it."

"I was in Milwaukee and got home today. Can we get together and talk about it?"

"That is why I called. Sven and I are in need of a ride to Calvary Cemetery and Como Park today. If we could bum a ride, I'd take you to dinner and we could talk?"

"That would be perfect Ned. I'll go tell Sister Alexine I won't be here for dinner and I'll be back late. I'll be over to the bakery in about fifteen minutes to pick you up."

They went over to the cemetery first before it got dark. It had been a long time since Ned was able to see Suzie. He missed her a lot. In fact, he knew he would always miss her. Knowing he wouldn't be around for a while, he set it up with a florist to deliver flowers on all the days he instructed. He noticed there were a few more graves by her. 'More people to keep her company,' he thought.

The sun began to go down. "What do you think about Schroeder's, Father?"

“I’d like that Ned.” They made their way toward the car, Ned whistling on his way. Stopping he said, “We can go past Como and see the lake on the way.”

“I’ll drive slow.”

Sven said, “You had better, Father. Dat old Studabaker gonna fall apart!”

Father McCarthy laughed and said, “Tell the Bishop. I think he had it for twenty years before me!”

They stopped by the pavilion under the light by the boat house. There was no one there except the kid locking up the pedal boats. The three men got out and walked toward the water. Richard and Sven talked to each other about bowling and Ned went over by the kid. Looking out over the docks Ned asked him, “How long have you worked here, son?”

"Oh, about five years I guess."

"What's your name?"

"Joe."

"Well, Joe, do you like it?"

Hanging his head he said, "Naw, but my family needs the money."

Seeing his disappointment Ned said, "Your parents are probably very proud of you. I would be."

"Thanks, Mister." Joe closed the door, locked it up, picked up his bike, and peddled away waving at Ned.

After packing to leave on his last night in St. Paul, Ned looked out Sven's front window toward St. Bernard's. He saw the bowling alley where he had first gotten himself into trouble with the whole mess. He wondered if anyone even thought about his "gift" lately. He hadn't. In fact he wondered if he could even do it anymore. Sven had the radio going and the sports were on WCCO. "Sven have you got a newspaper from today?"

"Ya, sure, Ned. Right here." He handed it to Ned.

Opening it to the sports schedule he looked at the times. He saw that the Dodgers and Sox were playing in a pre-season game in Florida. It had already started so he wrote down the first thing that came to mind- Sox 4-3. "Sven, I'm going to bed. It's been a long day."

"Goodnight, Ned."

There was a knock at the apartment door leading to the front stairs. Sometimes someone in need asked Sven for a handout that way, so not thinking anything of it, Sven opened up and said, "Can I help you?" The door flew open and a thug with a gun came in and pointed it at Sven. "Vat do you vant?"

"Shut up. Where's the old man- Ned?"

"I don't know who you mean." The guy hit Sven with the gun and he went to the floor. The bully ran up the stairs. Running from room to room, it didn't take long to find Ned.

"Get up. Let's go!" shouted the guy to Ned.

Calmly, Ned asked, "Where to?"

Changing his demeanor and settling down a bit the man said, "You'll find out."

Ned picked up his coat, hat, and bag, and walked down the steps to the back door avoiding Sven. The man led him to the alley where a black Cadillac from NY was waiting. He shoved Ned into the back and threw the suitcase in the trunk. Then things went bad for the two thugs. The car wouldn't start. The guy tried it again. It just cranked and cranked and cranked. Then above the hood came a faint glow. It grew lighter and brighter, becoming an ever more distinct shape and form. As the three watched, Ned knew what it was. His angel was coming to the rescue! Before long, a bright white angel was standing on the hood. The light of his presence lit up the whole alley! The two Italian bad men were shaking in their seats and one made the sign of the cross. The one in the back with Ned said, "Let's run for the church!" He tried to jump out, but the thug's door wouldn't open. The angel said, "You may leave, Ned. Peace be with you." Ned's back door came open and the trunk popped up. He got out and walked with bag in hand back into the house.

After he was inside, the angel left. He could hear the sound of the Cadillac starting and the Godfather's men zooming off like frightened rabbits. Ned went to Sven. He was dazed and sitting upright. "Vat happen?" he said to Ned as Ned straitened him up.

Ned looked at his wound. It wasn't bad, just a bump on the side of his head. "Someone tried to kidnap me again."

"Oh," Sven said rubbing his head.

"But, I don't think that will happen anymore."

"Gud. All dees Italians making so much messes makes me nervous." Ned laughed and helped Sven upstairs.

Ned called Malone first thing in the morning before he left for the airport. He told him the whole story and how Hal had changed and let him go. But then, he told him about last night and the danger from the Godfather. "You mean they tried to get you again? How did you get away?"

"Oh. Let's just say an old friend came to the rescue."

"That's the kind of friend I'd like to have."

"You do Andy. You do."

Ned hung up the phone and went to see Sven. "Vhat is dis here you make Ned? I don't see you get up and make it."

"I couldn't sleep after all the commotion. It's a new cookie. It's my, "Malachi Angel Cookie". You see the shape?"

Sven cocked his head and said, "Oh ya, for sure! It tastes gud too!"

"Did you eat my cookies?" Ned slapped Sven on the arm and Sven laughed as he walked away and took off his apron. "I need to get ready and call a cab," said Ned.

Reluctantly Sven responded, "I know."

As the cab parked in front of the bakery, Ned and Sven said their goodbyes. "Can I come to see da bakery?"

"Come to see me anytime my friend. Montana is a beautiful place."

They gave each other a hug. Sven opened the door of the cab and threw Ned's bag into the back seat. Ned put his cane down hard to brace himself as he grabbed the door and got in. The cabbie asked, "Where to?"

"The airport." They drove off away from the bakery, Rice Street, and for Ned, to a new way of life.

Chapter Thirty-Two- Ned Loses-but wins!

When he got on the plane the stewardess handed him a newspaper to read on the flight. He sat down in his seat and began to flip through the pages. Curiously, he looked at the sports scores. There on the bottom were the results of the Sox and Dodgers game. It read, "Dodgers win 3-2." The "gift" was gone. He hoped Malachi was not. Ned also hoped he wouldn't get a call from Hal asking him to place another bet. Somehow he knew that would not have to happen.

Ned got off the plane in Billings with a sense of new adventure. He lifted his vest pocket pulled out the chain and flipped open his new watch. Looking at it he said, "Time for a change". In fact, he had told Patsy to send Mulvaney Motors a draft for a used car for him to be waiting at the airport. He had not driven for years. Not since before the war. He was glad that he was in Montana and the traffic would be light! A man in a suit came up to him and said, "Are you Mr. Oelker?"

"Yes. I'm Ned."

"If you'd follow me, I have a car waiting for you out front."

After picking up his baggage, the salesman led him out to his new car. Ned loved the used Chevrolet sitting at the curb and he was all smiles. It was a 1940 yellow two-door with a brown pin-stripe. The tires looked –new! And it was an automatic! That's what he needed. He got in and started it up. "Not bad," he said out loud. "Thanks for bringing it up for me," he told the man leaving him at the curb and driving away. 'I wonder if he needed a lift?' he thought.

Ned had asked the realtor that Helmut had used, Tom Higham, to find a home for him while he was gone. He had left the purchase totally up to him, up to fifty-thousand. That much would get him any place in town! When he got to Red Lodge, he stopped at the realty office to find out where he was to live. He went in and Tom greeted him. "I think you'll like it, Ned. It's on the creek and I spent very little of your money."

"That's nice, but what's it like?" asked Ned.

"Come with me. I'll take you there."

They drove out past the edge of town and the road to Bear Creek. Going out a ways toward the National Forest, Tom stopped and pointing said, "There Ned- is your new home."

From the outside it looked like what Ned had wanted; a rustic log home. "Let's go see the inside," he said.

When he went in the door the first thing he wanted to see was the kitchen. Going straight there, Ned saw the wonderful huge open kitchen floor plan with an open-beam ceiling. In it was a wood burning stove with all the accessories! Next to it sat a four burner modern electric stove as well. Ned was in seventh-heaven!

On Sunday, May 6th, Ned went to church. He got there kind of late and saw where Sandy and Jim were sitting, and took a place by them. Looking toward the front, he saw Frieda sitting there with who Ned thought was her family. He'd find out more about that later, he thought. At least he hoped so! He wondered what Father McCarthy would say about his attending a Lutheran church. When service was over, everyone was talking about the news from Europe. It was said that the war would be over soon. Ned kept silent about what he knew there. He only smiled and said to someone, "It may be over sooner than we think!"

Frieda came up to him. "Hello, Ned. This is my son, Arville Swoboda."

Arville said to him, "Nice to meet you, Sir. Welcome to the community. My mother says you just bought the bakery. Would you like to come to dinner at my house today?"

"Thank you. Nice to meet you too, Arville. I'd love to come for dinner."

After church, Ned drove straight home. He was excited to be invited to the Swobodas' for dinner. He did not know what he would say or what he would do, but he thought it would be right to just be- himself. However, he thought it would be wise to dress a little different than for church. Ned didn't own a pair of blue jeans. So, he decided to wear a casual suit he used to wear when he went to the bowling alley. Not the Ritz, but it didn't need to be. So, to be ready, he laid it out on the bed. He ate lunch early, took a nap in a comfy chair, and got up at four. He was nervous, so he took a bath. It calmed him down a bit and then he figured he may as well get dressed for dinner.

Going out to the car, which he kept in the garage, he opened the garage door. In ran a dog! Surprising him, they both came to a standstill. They summed each other up for a second and then the dog calmly walked over to Ned, wagging his tail as he came. Ned said, "Well, hello. What's your name?" Not finding a tag on the beagle, he assumed it was a stray that had wandered off or got separated from its owner. Ned got in his car and backed out of the garage. The dog followed. After closing the door, Ned said to him, "If you're still here when I get back, you can stay." The dog sat down on the porch while Ned drove away.

Ned was escorted into Arville's house by his daughter, Penny. She took his hat and coat and said, "Please go on into the dining room. They are all in there," and she pointed down the hall to the left.

The house in the center of Red Lodge was one of the few Victorian era houses ever built there. The woodwork was exceptional and it reminded Ned of some of the homes he had seen in the Summit Hill area of St. Paul. He heard them all talking as he rounded the corner and Arville welcomed him immediately. "Welcome to my home, Mr. Oelker."

"No need to be so formal, Arville, please call me Ned." They exchanged a handshake and Arville showed him to a chair.

Ned sat down and Frieda came over to him from towards the kitchen. She asked, "I hope you like beef? We serve a lot of that here out west!"

The group laughed. “We have been in the beef business for years, Ned,” said Arville, “in fact, we own about 10,000 acres all around Red Lodge.”

Ned could only say, “I like beef almost as much as bread!”

The crowd laughed again and became at ease with him as a guest. By the time the meal was over and Ned was about to leave it was almost ten pm. He thanked his host and made his way to the door. Frieda brought his hat and coat to him. “Thank you for coming tonight, Ned.”

“I thank you all for allowing me to get to know your family and for Arville’s hospitality. I would like to do it again sometime. Next time at my place?”

Taking his hand Frieda smiled and said, “I would like that, Ned.”

When he got home the dog was still there. He pulled the car into the garage and the dog calmly walked over to Ned wagging her tail. She put her nose up in the air looking to be petted. Ned smiled and bent down to pet the dog. “OK, come on. Lets’ go inside and I’ll get you something to eat.” The dog followed him in. Taking off his coat and hat, he looked for a hook to throw his hat toward- nothing there yet. He said, “Gotta get me a hook.” So, he put them in the closet and the dog just sat at his feet when he sat down at the table. Ned looked down and asked her, “What am I going to call you? How about- Angel?” The dog didn’t react to that. He said, “OK. Angel it is.” Ned gave her some of the leftovers in the fridge as he didn’t have dog food around. The dog ate them like she hadn’t had anything for quite some time. “Poor girl. I hope that does the trick until I get you some food tomorrow.”

Ned’s phone rang. It was a party line, but Ned had the best ring, one long. He picked it up and said his familiar, “Hallo, this is Ned.”

“Hello, Ned, this is Sandy. Welcome back.”

“Hi Sandy! Glad to be back. Tomorrow I open my bakery. Come into town and see what I have done with it.”

“I wouldn’t miss it for the world.”

“How are Jim and the rest of the gang?”

“Just fine, Ned. Busy getting the herd moved and ready for spring.”

“Glad to hear it. Thanks for calling. See you tomorrow!”

“Bye, Ned.”

Ned hung up the phone and got ready for bed. He said a special prayer thanking God for the blessings of his life and the amazing outcome of the past few months, and not only that, but also for Malachi.

The next day, Hal and Tony sat on the veranda sipping coffee. “Man this coffee is good, Boss!”

“Yes it is. I’m thinking of buying some with my winnings.”

“Some? Boss?”

“Yeah, like the whole factory!” They laughed.

“I think I like Argentina, Boss.”

“So do I. All the best convicts, mobsters, and Germans come here! But it’s time to go straight. Ned taught us that.”

“Sure did, Boss. Sure did.”

“I think I’ll call it –“Heavenly Coffee Company”. What do you think, Tony?”

“I think Ned would approve.”

When Ned woke and turned on the radio, he heard Walter Winchell say on the news, “Today, May 7th, 1945, the Nazis surrendered!” He started to try to jump up and down, waving his cane in the air, he was so excited. He could hardly wait to get to the bakery. When he went outside, Angel followed him onto the porch. Ned and Angel got in the car and headed into town. What a way to start the day! Even though it was early people were all over the streets. All the shops were lit up and people were flying the flag and setting off fireworks. The crew all gave him a hug when he came in and they all talked about the war being over in Europe. Angel just came in and found a corner to lay down in, by the oven, where it was warm. Now they needed to end the Pacific theater. Ned said a prayer about that.

As he put on his apron and went to see the temperature in the oven, he looked inside. Standing in the fire he thought he saw someone. It was Malachi standing right there in the oven at 350 degrees! He said to Ned, "God has heard your prayer, Ned. The war will be over soon by a ball of fire. I will be there if you need me, Ned. Welcome to your new home. Oh, and I like your new dog." And then he was gone.

The door to the bakery opened and the cow bell rang. Ned knew it was to be his first customer. He came to the counter, smiled, and said to the woman, "Good morning and welcome to the Red Lodge Bakery."

Smiling back and then looking in the case she said, "I'll have one of those wonderful looking Angel Cookies. Are they sugar cookies?"

"Yes, I call them my Malachi Angels. And I'm not telling anyone what the secret ingredient is!"

"Oh! A secret ingredient! Wait until I tell the ladies!"

When she went out the door, the employees came out from the back smiling, and they all clapped as Ned stuck the first dollar on the wall with a pin. He picked up his cane from its logical resting place on the side of the new bakery case. Walking to the front door, he looked out Main Street across the wide Big Sky. "Suzie would like this," he said. Ned was finally home.

–The End-

Credits

Photographs from- MNHS-345 Kellogg Blvd. West, St. Paul, MN 55102-1906

Page 14- Washington High School and surrounding area, 1031-1041 Marion, St.Paul, MN. IRN: 100099195

Page 31- St. Bernard's Catholic Church, 197 West Geranium Street, St. Paul, MN IRN: 10202074

Page 62- Interior, Tschida Bakery, 1116 Rice Street, St. Paul, MN IRN: 10107506

Page 132- Tschida Bakery, 1116 Rice Street, St.Paul, MN IRN: 10097604

Page 170- Como Park pavilion, St.Paul, MN IRN: 10123405

About the Author

Craig A. Fiebiger, a native of Roseville, Minnesota, attended Eastern Montana College in Billings, Montana, now MSU-Billings. Receiving his BA in History, with a minor in Philosophy in 1987, he has gone on to become a man of many talents and wears many hats.

Besides pursuing writing as a career, he has been a plumber and contractor for over 40 years. Currently, he runs a small business in Thompsons Station, Tennessee.

He has also gone on to study theology and received his license and certificate as a Deacon in the LCMS, Mid-South District, where he now serves at his own congregation and others in the circuit as requested.

He enjoys fly-fishing, numismatics, golf, and metal detecting at civil war sites.

He currently resides in the Nashville, Tennessee area with his wife Shirreen and daughter Tara. He has two older children, Gary and Candace, and four grandchildren.